CONTAMINATION

JOHN VORNHOLT

Abridged and adapted by Joanne Suter

GLOBE FEARON
EDUCATIONAL PUBLISHER
PARAMUS, NEW JERSEY

Paramount Publishing

Globe Fearon Educational Publisher, a division of Paramount Publishing, 240 Frisch Court, Paramus, New Jersey 07652. No part of this book may be reproduced or transmitted in any form or by any means, electrical or mechanical, including photocopying, recording, or by any information storage and retrieval system, without permission in writing from the publisher.

Printed in the United States of America
1 2 3 4 5 6 7 8 9 10 99 98 97 96 95 94

ISBN: 0-835-91107-1

GLOBE FEARON
EDUCATIONAL PUBLISHER
PARAMUS, NEW JERSEY

Paramount Publishing

CONTENTS

CHARACTERS

Crew of the *U.S.S. Enterprise*

Beverly Crusher—doctor

Wesley Crusher—son of Beverly Crusher; not-yet full ensign on the bridge crew

Data—Lieutenant Commander and android; serves as the *Enterprise*'s science officer and helmsman

Guinan—hostess of the *Enterprise*'s Ten-Forward lounge

Geordi La Forge—chief engineer

Miles O'Brien—transporter chief

Jean-Luc Picard—Captain

William Riker—Commander and first officer

Deanna Troi—Counselor

Worf—Klingon Security Chief

Other characters

Lynn and Emil Costa—famous Federation scientists who are also husband and wife

Dr. Gastrow—scientist who works with the Costas

Shana Russel—assistant to the Costas

Saduk—Vulcan scientist working with the Costas

Fear. Anger. Pain. The feelings struck Deanna Troi like a fist. She could not help but pull back from the woman sitting across from her. Lynn Costa clawed both hands through her red and silver hair. Her thin shoulders—bent from hours spent over a lab table—shook with rage.

"How dare he put me here!" she screamed.

"Dr. Milu is just following rules," Deanna said calmly. "After you destroyed records, he had to do that. Can you explain why you did it?"

"They were *my* records from *my* project!" the woman hissed. "How long do I have to stay here?"

"This isn't a prison cell," said the ship's counselor. "I thought you might want to talk about what's troubling you, Dr. Costa."

"Don't you know? You're a Betazoid!" said the scientist. "Can't you read minds, like Dr. Milu?"

"I can sense feelings," Deanna said. "I'm not a full Betazoid like Dr. Milu. Even he can't read minds. He can communicate with his mind."

"Who cares?" shouted the woman. She leaned across the desk. "A two-year-old could read my mind. *I want off this ship!*"

Deanna sighed. She didn't care if Lynn Costa was a famous Federation scientist. The woman needed help. She needed to be quiet and listen to reason.

And those were the very words Deanna said. "Dr. Costa. Be quiet. Listen to me."

Surprisingly, the scientist did just that. She sank back in her chair and stared at Deanna. Then she began to sob. "Emil is leaving me," she cried.

At that moment, Lynn Costa looked more like a child than a woman nearing eighty years of age. Deanna could hardly believe that this person, along with her husband, Emil, had been leading the well-known Microcontamination Project. Their marriage was science's most famous partnership.

"How long have you been married?"

"Forty-eight years," the scientist whispered.

"Why is he leaving you?"

"He says he wants to quit working. He wants to go to Switzerland." She laughed coldly. "We worked so hard to get away from Earth and into space. Now he wants to go back."

"Why not enjoy yourselves? You and your husband have earned a rest. After all, you discovered the biofilter—"

"The biofilter, again!" shouted Dr. Costa. "Why does everyone talk about the biofilter? That was long ago. We've done many things since then!" She began to sob. "I thought coming to the *Enterprise* would be the best move of our lives. Instead, its been our downfall!"

Deanna felt she could do little to save the doctor's career. But she could work on saving her forty-eight year marriage.

"You and Emil should take time off together, just the two of you," she said.

"Yes!" cried the scientist. Suddenly she looked happier. "We must get off the ship—as soon as possible. But where?"

"You're in luck," Deanna answered. "In a few days we'll arrive at a new starbase. It is on a giant asteroid called Kayran Rock. It's the first starbase built on an asteroid and should be an interesting place to visit. The *Enterprise* is staying only for the base's grand opening. I'm sure you and your husband could stay longer."

Dr. Costa grabbed Deanna's jacket. "Do what it takes. You must get us off this ship. Before—"

"Before what?" asked Deanna. She was alarmed by the strong feeling of fear. "What are you afraid of?"

Lynn Costa pulled back. "I must return to the lab," she said. She hurried toward the door, and it whooshed open.

Deanna called after her, "Dr. Costa! Let me set up a meeting for both you and your husband."

The woman stopped in the doorway. She turned to Deanna with frightened eyes. "Just get us off this ship." Then the door slid closed behind her.

Deanna turned on her computer. "Counselor's log, stardate 44261.3," she slowly began her report. "I met with Dr. Lynn Costa. Our meeting was set up by her boss, Dr. Karn Milu. According to Dr. Milu, Lynn Costa has been acting strangely for weeks. She has destroyed computer records and lab notes. Dr. Costa has given no reasons for her acts. I noted that she is troubled, angry, and very much afraid of something."

Deanna turned to her food slot and asked for some hot tea. With the cup in hand, she continued. "I believe Dr. Costa should have time away from her work. It would be best to arrange a stay for her and her husband on Kayran Rock. Perhaps after some time, they will be able to return to work here or elsewhere in the Federation. I also suggest that Lynn Costa have a complete medical examination."

Deanna leaned back in her chair. "That is all." She sipped her tea. She hoped Captain Picard and Commander Riker would agree to leave the Costas on Kayran Rock. A couple needed to get away together sometimes. What would it be like, she wondered, if she and Will Riker could escape to a place like Kayran? She sighed and rose from her chair. She put the teacup back into the food slot. Then she turned down the lights and left the room.

The turbolift opened onto the lowest deck of the ship. Chief Security Officer Worf stormed out.

Several members of the engineering crew turned to stare at the Klingon. "What is it, Worf?" asked Geordi La Forge, the chief engineer.

"We held a security drill this morning," growled Worf. "It was slow, too slow. It took two minutes and sixteen-point-two seconds to get my officers from the bridge down here to engineering."

"Worf, that is as good as could be expected," said Geordi. "That's thirty-five decks to travel. How could you improve that?"

"We were in the turbolift one minute and forty-eight-point-three seconds!" snapped Worf. "Turbolifts should be faster than that!"

"They can be set to go faster," said La Forge. "But people would pass out or be pinned to the ceiling after ten or twenty decks. You forget, Worf, not everyone is as tough as a Klingon."

The bumps on Worf's forehead wrinkled in thought. "I don't want people to black out going to the Ten-Forward lounge, but we need to speed up the turbolifts in case of an emergency. You can do that, can't you?"

Geordi rolled his sightless eyes behind the VISOR he wore. "Yes, I can. But you'd better get a security team with strong stomachs."

Worf nodded. "Let me know when we can test it."

Guinan smiled at the man and woman seated at the table. As hostess of the Ten-Forward lounge it was her job to make everyone feel welcome. And Dr. Emil Costa had become one of her best customers.

She set an orange juice down and the old scientist growled his thanks. He scratched his short, white beard. His hair was hardly longer than the beard. His color was pale but not unhealthy looking. As usual, he pulled out a tiny blue bottle. He added something to the orange juice.

The lady with Dr. Costa was not his wife. Guinan could not place her, although she'd seen her before. "I'm Guinan," she said, holding out her hand. "I don't believe we have met."

The woman smiled. "I'm Shana Russel," she said shyly.

"She's only been on the ship for six months," said Emil Costa with just a hint of a German accent. "She's fresh out of school."

Guinan gave Shana a grin. It was always nice to have someone new to chat with aboard the *Enterprise*. "I'll be around if you need anything," she said. Then she moved off to other customers.

Deanna Troi and Commander Will Riker were at their own table in Ten-Forward. Deanna's voice was getting louder as she talked.

"Will, I just don't see how beaming Lynn and Emil Costa to a starbase will hurt relations with the Kreel," she argued.

"The Kreel have been at war forever, much of the time with the Klingons. They are not an easy people to get along with. Now they are letting the Federation build a starbase in their home solar system. It's a big step for them.

"But," he continued, "the Kreel don't have transporter technology. They want us to simply hand it over to them. We think they should develop it on their own. We've decided that everyone should go to Kayran Rock by shuttlecraft rather than by transporter. The shuttlecraft will be full. That is why only invited guests will be going."

"Then get the Costas invited," Deanna insisted.

"Only three people have been invited from the *Enterprise*," said Will. Captain Picard, Data, and myself. There isn't much room on the shuttle."

"Isn't there anything you can do?" asked Deanna. "The Costas really need some time alone."

Will squeezed her slim shoulder. "You are such a romantic," he said. He let his hand rest a moment longer. "I'll do what I can. Have the Costas ask for shore leave."

"Thank you." She smiled, touching his hand. Their eyes met and she read his feelings: caring, warmth, but also ambition. He wanted to be the captain of a starship someday.

Will pulled his hand away slowly. "I've got to get going. I'll see you on the bridge."

Guinan stopped at the table just as Riker was

leaving. She bent over Deanna. "Did I hear you mention Emil Costa?" she asked. "He's over there."

Deanna rose quickly. She walked to the doctor's table. "Hello, Dr. Costa," she said.

"Hello, Counselor Troi," Emil Costa mumbled. "This is one of our assistants, Dr. Shana Russel."

The young woman smiled cheerfully.

"How are things on deck 31?" asked Deanna.

"You should know," answered Emil Costa. "Don't you talk often with Dr. Milu?"

"Not really," said Deanna.

"You're a Betazoid, too!" Shana exclaimed. "This is so wonderful being aboard a ship with Vulcans and Betazoids and even a Klingon."

"Shana," said Dr. Costa, "the counselor and I have some things to talk about alone. Why don't you visit with Guinan at the bar for awhile"

Shana stood up and put out her hand. "Pleased to meet you, Counselor Troi," she said.

As soon as Shana had moved away, Emil Costa sighed. "Sorry, but I didn't want her to hear your report. She looks up to my wife."

"I don't really have a report," said Deanna. "Your wife talked to me for just a few minutes. Dr. Costa, do you know what she could be afraid of?"

"I don't know," the microbiologist growled.

He's lying, thought the ship's counselor, *and he's hiding something.* "I have suggested that the two of you take some time off when we reach the new starbase on Kayran Rock. Would you go?"

"Of course!" Emil exclaimed. He smiled for the first time. "That would be the perfect answer."

Deanna noted that both Emil Costa and his wife wanted off the ship very badly. "Commander Riker wants you to ask for shore leave in writing."

"We shall!" said the doctor. "Thank you!"

Emil Costa may have been happy, but Deanna wasn't. The perfect answer, he had said. The perfect answer to what? What was Emil Costa hiding?

The Betazoid did not sleep well during her rest period. She turned down the lights until the room was black. But she could not clear her thoughts.

At last, with the wild-eyed, wild-haired picture of Lynn Costa in her mind, Deanna drifted off to sleep. But she was troubled by a dream. In it, she wore a white suit and a white helmet. Her own breathing sounded in her ears. Sweat formed on her neck. She felt trapped.

Through the helmet she saw a white room. A row of metal pods stood in front of her. Each was just large enough for a human to fit inside. Gray windows showed tiny bottles and test tubes. The pods looked familiar, yet frightening.

In her dream, Deanna was drawn to the first pod. Something was wrong with it, she knew. She peeked through the gray glass. Suddenly a stream of yellow gas came from a valve on the outside of the pod.

She knew she had to run. The valve broke before she could turn away. The gas filled her eyes, nose, and mouth. Her eyes burned. She gagged. The suit was not meant to keep the air out, and the yellow gas poured in. It filled her helmet. She tried to stay on her feet, but the fight was already over. She was dying.

Deanna sat up in bed, gasping for breath. Her hair was soaked with sweat. She pushed a button beside her bed, and the lights came on. She rushed to the food slot and punched up a glass of water.

Suddenly, the familiar voice of Dr. Beverly Crusher came over the ship's communicator.

"Crusher to Troi. Are you awake, Deanna?"

Deanna took a deep breath. She calmed herself before answering. "Troi here. I'm very much awake."

"I'm sorry to bother you during your sleep period. It's about Dr. Lynn Costa."

Deanna was shaking. "What about Dr. Costa?" she asked. "Did you read my report?"

"Yes," answered Dr. Crusher. "Can you please come to sickbay?"

"Why?" breathed Deanna.

"Lynn Costa is dead."

CHAPTER 2

Deanna Troi ran from the turbolift into sickbay. She saw Dr. Beverly Crusher standing beside a slim body on a table. A steady hum came from the panel on the wall. Deanna knew the flat sound meant that the person on the table was dead.

Two men stood beside Dr. Crusher. One was Jean-Luc Picard, the captain of the *Enterprise*. The other was a huge human-looking creature who towered over everyone in the room.

"How did it happen?" asked Captain Picard.

Beverly Crusher nodded to the giant creature. "You should ask Dr. Grastow," she said. "He discovered the body."

Grastow was big but baby-faced. He had smooth, pink cheeks and a soft yellow beard. Deanna could see tears welling in his puffy pink eyes.

"We beamed Dr. Costa directly here," said Beverly Crusher. "But it was too late."

It was then that Deanna noticed the white suit on the floor. It was like the one in her dream.

Grastow followed her look. "The suit filters air flowing out, not coming in," he explained. "It's a clean room suit. It is meant to keep the room safe from the wearer's germs. It is not meant to keep the wearer safe from the air in the room." Then he began to sob. "Oh, this is terrible! I can't believe it!"

As the others waited for the giant to calm himself, the sickbay doors slid open. Commander Riker, Lieutenant Worf, and Lieutenant Commander Data rushed in.

Picard turned to them. "Is the clean room sealed off?"

"All rooms on deck 31 are self-sealing, Captain," answered Worf.

"The air in the room should be cleaned up in about two hours. It will be safe to go in then," said Dr. Grastow, pulling himself together.

"It's important we know what happened," said Worf.

"Of course," answered Grastow. "I haven't gone into the room yet, but I can tell you what I think happened. Lynn was working with dangerous gasses. Because the gas was deadly, she had it locked inside the pod. The way the gas was streaming out, I would guess that a valve or seal broke."

He shook his head. "I was working in the next lab and heard the alarm. When I got to the window, I saw Lynn just lying there—and I saw the gas. I called sickbay." The giant's voice choked with sobs. "I'll be happy to answer more questions later," he said. "Just now—I need to be alone."

"Of course," said Picard. Dr. Grastow nodded. Then he left the room, ducking through the doorway.

Will Riker looked after him. "They grow them big on Antares IV," he said.

"He is, in fact, small-to-average for an Antarean," Data informed them.

Captain Picard looked down at the figure on the table. "Has anyone told her husband?"

"No," said Beverly Crusher.

Jean-Luc frowned. It was a part of the captain's job he hated.

"Commander Riker," he said, "you schedule the funeral. Mr. Worf, I'm counting on you to inspect the cleanroom and the pod as soon as it's safe."

"May I go with you to see Emil Costa?" asked Deanna.

Jean-Luc nodded. "I could use your company, Counselor."

"Deck 32," Captain Picard told the computer as the turbolift door closed. "Deanna," he said, "how could this happen? We've always been so careful."

Deanna looked at the captain. He had been so proud to have the Costas aboard. He admired their work, and he admired their long-term marriage. Deanna hated to give him the next bit of news.

"Captain, the Costas's marriage was going very

badly. In fact, they were just about to leave the *Enterprise* because of it. I only found out about this a few hours ago. They were hoping to leave the ship at Kayran Rock."

The door of the turbolift opened onto deck 32. Most of the crew members living there were scientists who worked on deck 31. Deanna and Jean-Luc walked down the hall. They stopped when they came to a door with a sign reading, "The Costas." Captain Picard stiffened as he prepared himself for his unhappy job.

A slurry mumble answered his signal.

"What is it?"

"It is Captain Picard," said Jean-Luc. "I need to speak to you, Dr. Costa."

"I'm not in any shape for guests," came the voice. The words were followed by a few groans.

"This can't wait," said Picard. "It's about your wife."

The door slid open. A bleary-eyed little man stared at them. He wobbled on his feet.

Captain Picard took a deep breath and spit out his unhappy news. "Your wife has had an accident. Dr. Costa, she is dead."

Emil Costa blinked at them. "No," he shook his head. "She's working upstairs in the lab—some silly project."

"That's where the accident happened," said

Deanna. "Lynn was dead by the time her body was beamed to sickbay."

"No!" Emil Costa screamed. He slammed the door on them.

Deanna tried to recall what she sensed before he closed the door. There was no surprise. There was a great deal of fright, guilt, and sorrow.

"Did you smell alcohol on his breath?" asked Picard, moving away from the door.

"Yes," said Deanna.

Jean-Luc looked at her. "What's going on?"

Deanna shook her head. "Emil Costa is hiding something, and Lynn Costa was very troubled and scared. I think it's possible she killed herself."

"You say she was scared," said Picard. "Of what?"

"I don't know," Deanna answered.

"All right," Jean-Luc said. "You will go with Worf to the place she died. The two of you will find out exactly what happened."

"Yes, Captain," replied Deanna quietly. She was unhappy that she had not been able to help Lynn Costa. She did not especially look forward to working with Worf, but she forced a smile.

"Counselor," Picard said, "I know you and Worf haven't always seen eye-to-eye. He likes to get a job done quickly, and often doesn't stop to think about feelings while he's doing it. But he's the security chief on this ship. And you've talked to Lynn Costa.

You have some idea what was going on in her mind. I want a report from each of you. You will work together until we have some answers."

Worf glanced at Deanna Troi out of the corner of his eye. They were alone on the turbolift on their way to the science offices. There they would meet with Karn Milu, the head of the science department. Deanna was staring straight ahead. She seemed lost in her own thoughts. Worf would have been happier working on the case alone. But he knew that Deanna Troi had special talents.

The turbolift stopped. When the door opened, they found a thin Vulcan male waiting for them.

"I am Saduk," he said with a bow. "I work on the Microcontamination Project. I will show you where Dr. Costa's body was found. But first, Dr. Milu would like to see you."

"We'll follow you," said Worf. He liked dealing with Vulcans. They got right to the point.

Worf and Deanna followed the pointy-eared Vulcan to Milu's office. Its dark walls were covered with glass cases that held dead insects from throughout the galaxy.

The head scientist looked small behind his big desk. He was a short, square Betazoid with heavy eyebrows and a mass of gray hair. "Welcome," Dr. Milu said with a sad smile. "I wish your visit could be about more pleasant matters."

Karn Milu looked directly at Deanna. Tiny veins in his forehead throbbed. Worf could see Deanna step back a bit.

"Dr. Milu," she said, "I receive your thoughts but cannot send mine. And with Lieutenant Worf here, I think we should talk out loud."

"Of course," said the Betazoid scientist. "I only wanted to see if you have been practicing since our last meeting. I see you have not."

"To get right to our business," Worf broke in. "What can you tell us about Lynn Costa's accident?"

"Nothing," said Milu. "I have no idea what happened down there. I'm sorry I can't be more helpful. Unlike Counselor Troi, I try to tune out the emotions of the crew members and think only about my work."

"Who might know something?" asked Worf.

"Saduk has been with the Microcontamination Project longer than anyone except the Costas." Dr. Milu pointed to the Vulcan. "He'll show you around the lab. You should also talk to the two junior assistants, Grastow, the Antarean, and the Earth girl—" He snapped his fingers as if trying to think of her name.

"Shana Russel," said Deanna.

"Shana Russel," Milu repeated. "And of course you will want to talk to Emil."

Worf turned to the Vulcan Saduk. "When can we see the clean room?"

"Right now," nodded Saduk. He led them out the door.

As they moved down the halls of deck 31, Worf kept the Vulcan talking. "You do a great job here," he said. "No Klingon ship would have work areas as clean as these."

"Living beings are covered with germs, dust, and more. The biofilter cleans the air, but crew members bring contaminants in every time they enter a room. Clean room suits are the best way to keep a work area safe from the wearer.

"Which is why Lynn Costa's suit didn't save her," said Deanna.

"Yes," the Vulcan nodded. "The air *leaving* the suit was highly filtered. The air entering the suit was not."

The Vulcan stopped in front of a door. "The pods are in a class-one clean room. Special clean room suits are a must." He spoke clearly. "Saduk requesting entrance."

"Voice-print matched," replied the computer. The door slid open.

They entered a white hall. Suddenly they were struck by a breeze of cool air. "An air shower," explained Saduk, "to blow off contaminants."

Along one wall was a rack of white suits and a pile of helmets. At the end of the hall were three doors. Each was marked with a sign:

MICROCONTAMINATION, MEDICAL, MANUFACTURING.

"Once you put on the suits, you will be free to enter the clean rooms," said Saduk.

They each took a clean suit from the rack. Deanna was surprised the white cloth was so light. The suit flowed comfortably over her own clothing. The helmet was another story. As soon as Saduk snapped it over her head, Deanna felt closed in.

Saduk snapped on his own helmet. "This way," he said. His voice echoed from inside the helmet.

The scientist opened the door marked **MICROCONTAMINATION** and led them into a white room. Deanna realized that it looked exactly like the room in her dream. There was the row of pods with their gray windows. Suddenly, she was filled with the same fear she had felt in her dream. "Is it safe for us to be here?" she gasped.

"The room is clean again," said Saduk.

Deanna felt the uneasy silence. She saw the cold pods. To her, the lab seemed like a tomb.

Each pod had its own computer screen. Most of the screens were lit, but the screen beside pod number one was dark. "We'll check the seals before we use the pod again," said Saduk.

Worf looked closely at the valves and the seals. "It seems the equipment has been kept in perfect shape," he said. "This appears to be a very unlikely accident."

While Worf and Saduk were examining the seals, Deanna glanced around the room. Something on the floor caught her eye. In the spotless laboratory, the small, blue bottle seemed out of place. She reached down with a gloved hand and picked it up.

"Look at this," Saduk was saying to Worf. "This valve may appear to be all right, but it's not. Notice the strange marks on the seal. This valve was sure to fail."

"Are you saying that someone tampered with the valve?" asked Worf

"Yes," said the Vulcan dryly. "Lynn Costa's death was no accident. Someone killed her."

"Could it be possible that Dr. Costa killed herself?" asked Deanna.

"Yes," said Saduk. "She had as much chance as anyone to tamper with this equipment. Surely she could have ended her life in easier, less painful ways."

Deanna closed her hand around the blue bottle. Should she ask about it? Not at the moment, she decided.

Worf pounded a gloved fist into his other hand. "A murder on the *Enterprise*! I swear, the killer will be found!

CHAPTER 3

Worf and Deanna were happy to take off their white suits and helmets. Worf held the pod valve carefully. It would help prove that Lynn Costa's death was no accident.

Deanna looked at her own clue, the small blue bottle.

"Where did you find that?" asked the Vulcan, Saduk.

"Inside, near the pod," Deanna answered.

Worf held out his hand. Deanna gave the bottle to him. He put it under his nose. "Alcohol," he said. Then he tucked it away with the valve.

"Dr. Saduk," Worf said, "do you know anyone with something to gain from Lynn Costa's death?"

"I know one person," said the Vulcan. "Myself. With Lynn Costa dead and Emil Costa retiring, I will head the Microcontamination Project."

"Anyone else?" demanded Worf.

"No one comes to mind," the Vulcan replied.

"Saduk," said Deanna, "Lynn was caught erasing records. What sort of records had she erased?"

"Our team has discovered new germs on nearly every planet we've visited," said the Vulcan.

"Mainly she erased records of these microbe discoveries. She also destroyed some personal files and notes. It was quite strange."

"Don't talk about our investigation with anyone," Worf warned Saduk. "I'll be sending some engineers to go over that pod."

"Understood," said Saduk. "Can you find your way out?"

"Yes," said Deanna. "Thank you." She turned to Worf. "Well," she sighed. "We had better go see the captain."

Jean-Luc Picard shook his head. "Murdered!" he barked. "Are you absolutely certain?"

"No," Worf answered. "Not until we check this valve and prove it has really been tampered with. I will have Geordi and some engineers go over the pod. Saduk could be mistaken—or lying."

"No," said Picard, "a Vulcan who lied like that would have to be quite insane."

"Captain," said Deanna. "I doubt if I could tell if Saduk is lying or not. He has a very strong and well-guarded mind. He does have a motive. And, there is the chance that we are dealing with someone who is insane."

Captain Picard sighed. "You're right. We can't rule anyone out."

"If there is a murderer aboard the *Enterprise*,"

promised Worf, "I will find him!"

The captain nodded. Then he turned to Deanna. "Counselor, I hate using you as a lie detector, but we haven't got any choice. Can you go with Worf when he questions the suspects?"

"Yes, sir," replied the Betazoid. "I might have saved Lynn Costa if I had taken her fear more seriously. I want very badly to find out what happened to her."

"Make it so," Picard ordered.

As they stepped into the turbolift, Worf tapped his communicator. "Worf to La Forge."

"Geordi here," came the voice. "We've gone over the pod and that valve you gave me. The pod seems to be in perfect working order. The valve is a different story. It's been changed just enough to let the gas escape. Whoever tampered with it knew exactly what to do. It looks like an inside job to me. I'd take a closer look at those folks in the Microcontamination Project."

"We're doing just that right now," said Worf.

The turbolift door opened onto deck 32. "Which way to Emil Costa's cabin?" he asked Deanna.

"It's not far. Let me lead." Deanna started down the hall.

When Worf pressed the door chime, a serious— and sober—Emil Costa greeted them. He appeared old and tired. His eyes had a haunted look. The counselor remembered that same look in Lynn Costa's eyes.

"I wondered when you would come," the scientist said. He stepped back so they could enter. The quarters were simple and comfortable. A collection of cuckoo clocks dotted the walls.

Worf got right to the point. "We've come to tell you that we believe your wife was murdered."

Emil Costa fell into a chair. He seemed overcome, but not really surprised.

"Did you kill her?" asked Worf.

"We're not going to waste any time, are we?" Emil said. "No, I didn't."

"Do you know who did?" asked Worf.

"No," mumbled Costa.

He's lying, thought Deanna. The only problem was, which question was he lying about?

"Dr. Costa," said Deanna gently, "wouldn't you want to see your wife's killer punished?"

"Of course," said the scientist. "But really, what good is revenge. Oh," he cried, "I wish I were the one who was dead."

Even Worf felt sorry for the old man. But he had a job to do. "Did you tamper with the valve on pod one?"

"Is that how it was done?" sniffed Emil Costa.

"Why," asked Deanna, "did Lynn destroy the computer files of your microbe discoveries?"

The scientist turned away. "There is nothing I can tell you," he cried. "Please leave me now."

"We will want to talk again," warned Worf.

"You know where to find me," Emil replied. "I have left the Microcontamination Project. I will stay in my cabin."

Worf strode from the room. Deanna didn't catch up with him until he was halfway down the hall. "He's lying about something," she declared.

"Yes," Worf said. "He didn't want to talk about the erased files."

"He does seem truly broken up over his wife."

"More than one murderer has been sorry for his actions afterward," growled Worf. "Whom shall we see next?"

"Grastow," answered Deanna. "He discovered the body."

They stepped down into Grastow's cabin. The floor of the room had been lowered so the huge Antarean could fit. Worf led the way into the room. It was strange to see someone towering over the Klingon.

"How may I help you?" asked Grastow.

"We believe," said Worf, "that Dr. Costa's death was not an accident. The valve on pod number one had been tampered with."

"Do you have any suspects?" Grastow asked.

"To be honest," answered Deanna, "everyone is a suspect right now. Even you."

"Me?" exclaimed the Antarean. "Why would I kill Lynn Costa? I loved the woman!"

"Loved?" asked Worf.

"Loved, respected, admired," said Grastow. "It began when I was a boy. My home planet was attacked by microbes. These germs contaminated our soil and killed our crops. We were starving to death. It takes a lot of food to feed a planet full of Antareans.

"Anyway, the Costas spent a year of their lives working on the problem. They taught us how to clean the soil. They saved my planet. I promised myself I would thank the Costas. I became their assistant. Only Saduk has been with them longer than I have."

"Who do you think murdered Lynn Costa?" asked Worf.

"The pods," Grastow explained, "are in the Microcontamination clean room. That means that no one is allowed inside that room without a scientist from that project. Therefore, the best suspects are myself, Saduk, Shana, and Emil."

"Who do you think is most likely to have murdered the doctor?" Worf pressed.

"I hate to say it," said the Antarean, "but Emil is the likely choice. During the last few months, the two of them fought like tigers. A few times, I thought they would come to blows."

"Thank you for your help," said Worf. He was already starting for the door. Apparently, he thought there was little more to be learned from the Antarean.

"What do you think?" he asked Deanna when they were out in the hall.

The Betazoid shook her head. "I didn't sense he was lying. He seemed honest about everything he said. Of course, he may be able to block out negative thoughts. I might not be able to tell if he is lying."

Worf frowned. It seemed they were getting nowhere. "Who's next?" he asked.

"Shana Russel," said Deanna. She remembered the young woman she had seen in the Ten-Forward lounge with Emil Costa. "She's only been on the ship for six months."

"She could get into the clean room," said Worf. He tapped his communicator. "Computer? Is Shana Russel in her cabin?

"No, Lieutenant Worf," the female voice answered. "She is in the Ten-Forward lounge."

Worf held out his hand for Deanna to lead the way.

The Ten-Forward lounge was quiet when Deanna Troi and Lieutenant Worf entered.

"Hello," Guinan welcomed them. "I don't suppose you've come here to relax."

"We're looking for Shana Russel," said Worf.

Guinan pointed to a corner of the room. "She's been sitting there for hours."

The young blond was staring out the port at the stars.

"Excuse me," said Worf. "We have to speak to you."

"Yes," whispered Shana Russel. She looked up at him. Her yellow hair was stuck to cheeks wet with tears. Even Worf softened at the sight.

"May we sit down?" he asked with a bow.

"I'm Deanna Troi," said the Betazoid with a smile. "Do you remember me? We met earlier. I'm afraid you know why we're here now."

"Yes," Shana whispered. "I didn't feel like being alone in my room, so I came here."

"How much do you know about what happened to Lynn Costa?" asked Worf.

Shana shook her head. "Since I've been sitting here, I've heard some people talking. They say it wasn't an accident! Is that true?"

"We don't know," Worf answered gently. "That's why we're talking to people who could get into that clean room. Did you change any of the equipment on that pod?"

"On pod number one?" asked Shana, wide-eyed. "I wouldn't go near Dr. Costa's experiments unless she asked me to!"

"Someone did," said Deanna.

Suddenly the young scientist sat up straight. "You think I—!" she cried. "You're crazy!"

"We are asking everyone," Worf explained. "Do you know of anyone using that pod besides Dr. Costa?"

Shana Russel shook her head. She sank back into the chair and began to cry softly. Deanna touched Worf's shoulder and nodded toward the door.

Worf stood. "Sorry to have bothered you. If you think of anything, please come to me."

"She doesn't seem to know much," he told Deanna as they headed for the door.

"No," agreed Deanna unhappily. "No one does."

The Klingon reached into his pocket. He pulled out the little blue bottle. "I wonder if Shana Russel has seen this before."

"I have," said a voice behind them.

Worf and Deanna turned to see Guinan. "Let me look at that," the hostess said.

She took the bottle and sniffed its narrow opening. "I've seen it, or one just like it, right here. Emil Costa had it with him. He often carried it—to spice up his orange juice."

Worf and Deanna looked at each other. The Klingon's hands formed fists. Then he stormed out the door. Deanna had to run to catch up with him.

She finally stopped him at the turbolift. "That's not enough proof, Worf. You need more!"

The Klingon breathed heavily. "You are right," he

groaned. "We cannot go to Starfleet with this one clue. We have to find a reason for the murder. I think the next step is to look over all the records for the Microcontamination Project. We will check each staff member—starting with Emil Costa."

Ensign Wesley Crusher hid a yawn. The bridge was quieter than usual. Data was there, but he was busy scheduling the shuttlecraft for Kayran Rock. It must be a hard job, Wesley thought. He'd heard that all Klingon and Kreel visitors had to arrive at different times. Bad blood still existed between the two races, and the Federation didn't want any trouble. Data was sitting at his computer trying to figure it all out. Wesley knew better than to bother him.

The rest of the bridge crew seemed lost in their own thoughts. Lynn Costa's death had cast a sadness over the whole ship. It was too quiet.

Therefore, Wesley was glad when a message came over the communicator. "Worf to Ensign Crusher."

"Crusher here," answered the teenager.

"When you leave the bridge, I would like to see you," said the Klingon.

"Yes, sir," said Wesley, excitedly. He guessed that Worf's request had something to do with the investigation into Dr. Costa's death.

When he left his post, Wes hurried to Worf's security office. He entered to find all the computer screens aglow. Worf was watching the goings-on in many parts of the ship.

The Klingon turned to him."I have some undercover work for you," he said. "I see that Emil Costa used to tutor you in microbiology. Do you think you could renew your friendship with him?"

"Now?" cried Wesley. "But his wife just died!"

"Ensign, Emil Costa is the main suspect in this murder. Maybe you can clear him, maybe not. I want you to stay close to him, watch him, and find out if he killed his wife. Without letting him know, of course."

"But I'm his friend," said the teenager.

"Not on this assignment," replied Worf. "You are a detective. You are not to tell anyone. Is that understood?"

Wesley nodded.

"I will inform Captain Picard, Commander Riker, and Counselor Troi. No one else needs to know. Try to get close to him at the funeral," Worf suggested.

"Yes, sir," answered Wesley.

"Dismissed," Worf said. Then he called Wesley back. "You must never put yourself in danger. Remember, Emil Costa could be a murderer."

CHAPTER 4

Deanna Troi was awakened by the ring of her door chime. She shook her head to clear her mind of sleep. Then she wrapped her robe around her. She tossed her dark hair once before opening the door.

It was her fellow Betazoid, Karn Milu. "May I come in?" His voice sounded angry.

Deanna nodded and stepped back. "What is wrong?" she asked.

"It's Lieutenant Worf!" the scientist growled. "He has the science department in an uproar."

"I'm sorry," sighed Deanna. "But Worf has the hard job of finding a murderer."

"You show me proof that this is a murder," muttered Milu, "I haven't seen anything that says murder!"

"Saduk said—" Deanna began. But the scientist wouldn't let her finish.

"Saduk is wrong!" he snapped. "Don't tell me that a Vulcan always has to be right."

A question popped into Deanna's mind. "Is Saduk still in line to head the Microcontamination Project?" she asked.

"No," Milu said flatly.

"Is Grastow your choice, then?" asked Deanna.

"That's not your worry," answered Karn Milu. "Counselor, there will never be proof enough to turn this into a murder case. That is what you should be concerned about."

"Lieutenant Worf is in charge of this case," Deanna said. "He will do things as he sees fit."

At that, Karn Milu stormed angrily out of the room. Deanna shook her head. She could see that her countryman would offer little help in finding the truth.

Lieutenant Worf leaned back and rubbed his eyes. He and Deanna Troi had been staring at computer screens for what seemed like hours. After discussing Deanna's visit from Dr. Milu, they had been reading about the Costas's work.

"It's almost eighteen-hundred hours," said Worf. "Let's go over the information we've gathered. What have you found?"

Deanna tried to sum up all she'd read. "The Costas perfected a biofilter that could clean the air. With that discovery," she explained, "they won the respect of the Federation. They formed the Microcontamination Project and were given total control of their own research."

She brought up some information on her screen

and pointed to a name. "A woman named Megan Terry once sued the Costas. Terry claimed that *she* had perfected the biofilter while working with Lynn and Emil. She said that the Costas stole the idea and claimed it as their own. Megan Terry lost her suit twenty-five years ago. In fact, she's been dead for five years."

Deanna leaned back. "Other than that, the Costas have spent their whole lives on their research. They have no hobbies, outside of Emil's fondness for alcohol and cuckoo clocks." Deanna yawned. "That's about it. So what do we have for all our work?"

"Very stiff necks," growled Worf. The Klingon stood up and stretched. "I gave Wesley Crusher an undercover job, and I would like to give you one, too. At the funeral, try to get friendly with Saduk. See if he has learned anything new."

Deanna nodded. "I was already planning to do just that."

The funeral was held in the theater room of the *Enterprise*. Every seat was filled and crew members were standing in the aisles. Through a viewport, the stars glided past at warp three. But everyone's attention was on the silver casket in the center of the stage. It was aimed like a missile at the starry heavens beyond.

Commander Riker stepped up on the stage. He looked out at the sea of serious faces. Deanna was talking with a tall, slim Vulcan. Wesley Crusher stood next to Emil Costa. The old man's head was bent. From the Microcontamination Project, the big Antarean, Grastow, and the blond woman, Shana Russel, stood together. The captain was talking to Doctor Milu. Worf roamed through the crowd. His bony forehead moved like a shark's fin over the other heads.

Voices died down as Will Riker started to speak. "Thank you for coming to this service for Dr. Lynn Costa," he began. "It seems fitting that Dr. Costa will finally rest out in space. She spent much of her life working with the space around us. She found new ways to keep it clean and safe." Will cleared his throat. "I am only sorry that—and I'm sure I speak for many of us—we didn't get to know her better. But Lynn Costa gave her time and her talent to the Federation." He turned to the casket and smiled, "Lynn, we'll miss you, but we will remember you by all you have given us."

Commander Riker stepped down from the stage. Captain Picard took his place. "Normally in these cases," began a very serious Jean-Luc Picard, "the captain is supposed to say something comforting. But I do not feel comfortable about Lynn Costa's death."

The room fell totally silent. It seemed that no one was breathing. "I know," Jean-Luc continued, "this is a sad time. But we must deal with the problem before us. Lynn Costa's death should not have happened. So," he asked, "if anyone has any information, please see Lieutenant Worf, Counselor Troi, or myself."

Picard looked at the casket and shook his head. "We think people like Lynn Costa will live forever. They are as important to us as the sun is to a planet." He tapped his communicator badge. "Picard to transporter room."

"Yes, sir," answered the transporter operator.

"Energize," ordered the captain.

In a shower of lights, the silver casket disappeared. Most eyes in the room turned to the viewport and the stars beyond. There Lynn Costa's remains were scattered forever.

Wesley Crusher let out his breath. He turned to see how Emil was doing. But the white-haired scientist was gone.

Wes pushed his way to the door. Watching Emil Costa was his job. He wasn't about to let Worf down.

The security chief was also making his way through the crowd. "Lieutenant Worf?" a soft voice stopped him.

He turned to look down at the pretty face of

Shana Russel. The tiny female looked up from under a cloud of blond hair.

"Yes?" he answered hurriedly.

"I'm sorry I was so little help to you and Counselor Troi when we spoke in the Ten-Forward lounge. You were just doing your jobs. I know you have to question everyone." Her voice lowered to a whisper. "But I do have some information. I once heard someone threaten to kill Dr. Costa."

"Who?" asked the security chief. He expected to hear her name Emil Costa.

"Karn Milu," she breathed.

The Klingon blinked. "You heard this yourself?"

The young assistant looked around. "I don't want to talk here. Can we meet alone?"

"My office—" Worf began.

"More private than that," whispered Shana. "Come to my quarters on deck 32, cabin B-49."

Worf nodded.

Shana squeezed his arm. "Be sure to come alone," she added.

Worf headed for the captain's ready room. Picard had sent for him. His visit to Shana Russel would have to wait.

He found Picard and Data together in the ready room. "Come," Picard motioned to the Klingon. "I have some news for you. Starfleet has granted Emil Costa permission to get off the *Enterprise* at Kayran Rock," Picard explained. "He is leaving the ship permanently."

"Captain—" began Worf with concern.

Picard raised his hand. "Let me get back to this in a minute." He turned to the android. "Data, we need more speed to meet the Kreel ship on time. Six Kreel delegates will be riding our shuttlecraft to Kayran Rock. They will join you, Commander Riker, and myself. The remaining seat on the shuttle will be filled by Emil Costa. Now, increase speed to warp four. Dismissed."

"Yes, sir," answered Lieutenant Commander Data. He headed for the door.

"Data!" called Worf. "How long before the shuttlecraft leaves?"

"Four hours at the earliest," came the reply.

"Thank you," growled Worf, and the android was gone.

"I know you are not happy about this," Picard said to Worf. "Frankly, neither am I. The fact is, we have no right to keep Emil Costa here."

"Captain," barked Worf, "I'm sure we are about to uncover something. We found a blue bottle on the floor near the pod. It is just like the one that Emil Costa was carrying earlier."

"You have a clue," admitted Jean-Luc. "But you

have no real proof that Lynn Costa's death was anything but an accident."

"I can feel it," said Worf.

Picard shook his head. "Quite possibly Lynn Costa's death will always be a mystery."

"Captain," said Worf, "both Troi and I are sure it is murder. Give me the next four hours until Emil Costa leaves the ship. If we do not have enough to charge him by then, we will end the investigation."

"Very well," Picard sighed, "and Lieutenant, try to get some sleep. Commander La Forge will need you on the bridge while Data, Riker, and I are on Kayran Rock."

CHAPTER 5

Wesley Crusher hurried down the hall on deck 32. He wanted to catch up with Emil Costa. Why had the scientist suddenly disappeared at his wife's funeral, Wes wondered. If Emil had nothing to do with his wife's death, why was he acting so guilty?

Ensign Crusher stopped at the door marked "The Costas." He rang the chime. When the door opened, it wasn't the old scientist who met him. Instead, the giant Antarean filled the doorway.

"I am Ensign Crusher," said Wesley, stepping back. "I would like to see Dr. Costa."

The Antarean blocked the door. "I am Grastow," he said. "Dr. Costa is seeing no one. He is resting until it's time to leave on the shuttlecraft."

"I'd like to see him for just a moment," said Wesley. He took a step forward. But two big hands grabbed his shirt. Grastow pushed him against the wall, and the air shot out of his chest. When the hands let go, Wes slid down the smooth wall. He landed in a gasping pile on the floor.

"By Dr. Costa's order," warned the Antarean, "*no one* is to see him." He went back into the cabin. The door slid shut behind him.

Wesley stood in the hall for some time. He watched other crew members come to pay their respects to Emil Costa. Each time, Grastow answered the door. Each time he turned the visitor away.

Surely Dr. Costa would want to say good-bye to friends before leaving for Kayran Rock, thought Wesley. He began to wonder whether Dr. Costa was in that room at all.

There was one way to find out. All he needed was a tricorder. Wesley knew that a first-aid kit was placed in every hall of the *Enterprise*. And every kit contained a tricorder. He found the red box on the wall at the end of the hall. He opened it. A tricorder was among the bandages.

Wesley took the instrument and returned to Costa's cabin. He aimed it at the door and searched for signs of life within. The tricorder recorded only one life form. It was a large one, to be sure, but only one living being.

Just then the door slid open. A huge figure appeared. A meaty hand snatched the tricorder from Wesley's grasp. "What are you doing?" cried Grastow.

Wesley didn't wait around to answer. He turned and ran. Let Grastow keep the tricorder!

Putting two and two together had always been Wesley Crusher's strong point. He knew that Grastow was alone in Emil's cabin. Perhaps that meant that Emil was hiding in Grastow's cabin.

It didn't take long to find out that the Antarean also stayed on deck 32. Wesley hurried to Grastow's room. He banged on the door. "Dr. Costa," he shouted, "let me in! I know you're in there!"

On another part of deck 32, Lieutenant Worf was quickly making his way to Shana Russel's cabin. He had only four hours to find a murderer.

Worf chimed at Shana's door. It slid open, and the young woman pulled him inside.

"Good!" she breathed. "You came alone. I just don't know what to do. I'm so upset by all this." She blinked her blue eyes at Worf.

"Calm down," said Worf. "Now, what is it you wanted to tell me about Karn Milu?"

"Oh, that?" she sighed. "It was right after Lynn erased the computer records. I don't think they saw me. He was screaming at her."

"What exactly did he say?" asked Worf.

"He said very clearly, 'If you mess this up, I'll kill you.'"

Worf narrowed his eyes. "Mess what up?"

Shana shook her head. "I have no idea. All I know is he was very mad at her. This is so awful!"

Before Worf could step aside, the young woman hugged him around the chest.

"I'm afraid," she whispered. "Stay with me."

Worf gently pushed her away. "You are upset.

Perhaps, if you talked to Counselor Troi—"

"I don't want Counselor Troi," she breathed, trying to hug him tighter.

Worf held her at arm's length, gently but firmly. "This is a hard time for all of us. But we must think only of finding the truth. Thank you for your information."

"Of course," mumbled the girl. Her face turned bright red, and she smoothed her hair. Then she smiled hopefully. "Maybe when this is all over, we could have dinner together?"

"When this is all over," said Worf, "I plan to sleep for at least two shifts. Good-bye."

"Let me in!" Wesley yelled again. The door of Grastow's cabin slid open. A hand reached out and pulled Wesley Crusher inside. "Did you have to yell like that?" Emil Costa exclaimed.

"What are you doing, sir?" Wesley asked. "Why are you hiding?"

The old scientist shook his head. "It's a long story, Wesley," he sighed. "And besides, I am putting an end to the whole thing tonight, before I leave the ship. It will be over, once and for all."

"Do you know who killed your wife?" asked Wes.

Emil Costa held his head in his hands. "No!" he cried. "Oh! We brought it all on ourselves!" He began to sob loudly.

"Dr. Costa," said Wesley, "would you like to talk to someone, like Counselor Troi?"

"No!" gasped the old man. "Don't call any of your friends. Like I said, I will end this tonight. You must trust me, Wesley. Do nothing!"

The door suddenly opened. The huge Antarean came in. Wesley jumped back, but Grastow hardly noticed him. He rushed to Emil Costa's side.

"Doctor, are you all right?" he asked.

"Yes," smiled Emil. He patted Grastow's huge shoulder. "You have done well. Our young friend was just too smart for us."

Grastow looked at the teenager. "I'm sorry," he said. "I hope I didn't hurt you."

"I'm okay," said Wesley, rubbing his back. "I just wish I could help you, Dr. Costa."

"You can," said Emil. "Please don't follow me." Then the scientist walked over to the communicator on the wall. "Emil Costa to Karn Milu," he said.

"Milu speaking," replied the Betazoid. "Have you decided to talk?"

"I have," said Emil. "Where are you?"

"I'll meet you in the pod room. We can be alone there," answered Milu.

"Very well," Dr. Costa agreed. Wesley noticed that his hands were shaking.

"If you're going, Doctor," said Wesley, "then I will, too."

"No," said Emil. "I want you and Grastow to stay here."

At that, the big Antarean wrapped his arms around Wesley. He sat him down in a chair. Wesley reached for his communicator badge. Grastow was faster. He pulled the badge from Wesley's shirt, tearing off a piece of red cloth with it.

"Give that back!" cried Wesley. But his attention was not really on Grastow. He was shocked to see Emil Costa taking a phaser from a drawer by his bed. "Dr. Costa!" he shouted. "Where are you going with *that?*"

"One can't be too careful," answered the doctor. As the door opened, Emil Costa hid the phaser under his belt.

"No!" cried Wesley. But one huge hand was already covering his mouth. Another pressed him into the chair and held him there.

In the main shuttle bay, Commander Riker watched the Kreel delegation arrive. They climbed clumsily out of their own beat-up shuttlecraft. These have to be the ugliest beings in the galaxy, Riker thought. The Kreel had huge jaws and almost no necks. Long, skinny legs that looked as if they could not possibly hold up their big upper bodies. They wore few clothes over their hairy, red skin.

The Kreel shuffled awkwardly along with a side-to-side rocking motion.

"Greetings!" Riker called. He tried to sound cheerful. "I am Commander William T. Riker, first officer of the *Enterprise*. Welcome aboard!"

The six Kreel shuffled to a stop. One of them bowed. "I am Kwalrak," she said in a woman's voice, "assistant to Admiral Ulree of the Kreel Empire."

"I am Ulree," growled another Kreel. "There are no Klingons aboard, are there?"

Will paused. "One of our bridge officers is a Klingon. But he has other duties today."

"Cleaning the bathrooms, I imagine!" laughed a third Kreel. The others roared as if that were a great joke.

Riker sighed. "Would you like to learn more about our ship before we leave for Kayran Rock? Come with me."

The Kreel shuffled along behind him as he left the shuttle bay. Kwalrak, the female, moved uncomfortably close. She wrapped a leathery arm around his shoulder. "I would like to learn more about you, Commander Riker," she cooed. She bent her triangle-shaped head closer. "Follow us," she ordered the other Kreel delegates.

"Just because she's beautiful," Ulree muttered, "she thinks she can run things."

"Dr. Costa said we should stay here. He didn't say you should strangle me!" Wesley gasped at Grastow.

"You won't try to escape?" the Antarean asked.

Wes shook his head. "I'll sit quietly."

Grastow let go of Wesley. He placed himself in front of the door and watched the teenager.

"You know," coughed Wesley, "you could get in a lot of trouble for this."

"What happens to me is not important," Grastow said. "What counts is Emil Costa and his safety."

"What is he so afraid of?" Wesley asked. "And what does Karn Milu have to do with it?"

Grastow shook his head. "I don't know."

Wesley sat back quietly. He had noticed a light panel just to his left. If he could make the room totally dark, he might be able to get out. Wes began to plan his escape. Something would have to slow Grastow down. The chair he was sitting in might do. He would drag it behind him, tip it over, and leave it in Grastow's darkened path.

Wesley's heart beat faster. He looked at the Antarean. Grastow was less alert now. He even yawned.

Suddenly, Wesley sprang from the chair, giving it a hard pull. The chair hit the floor. His hands hit the light panel, and the room went black. He heard the Antarean shout and come after him.

In the dark, with fear pounding in his chest,

Wesley moved toward the door. He heard a cry like a wounded elephant as Grastow fell over the chair and crashed to the floor.

He felt for the door panel. As the door slid open, a hand grabbed at his foot. He jerked away and fell out into the brightly lit hall.

Wes got to his feet and rushed to the nearest communications panel. He pounded it.

"Ensign Crusher," he gulped. "to transporter room. Come in O'Brien!" He looked behind him to see the groaning Antarean crawling out of the cabin.

"O'Brien here," came a voice. "What can I do for you, lad?"

"Beam me directly to the clean room of the Microcontamination Project. It's on deck 31!" cried Wesley.

"What's the matter with the turbolift?" asked O'Brien.

Fire burning in his pink eyes, Grastow caught sight of Wesley. He rose up from the floor to his full height.

"Do it now!" barked the ensign. "I'm on a special job for Worf. It's a matter of life and death! *Energize!*"

The Antarean's arms wrapped around the sparkles of light. Wesley Crusher himself was gone.

The ensign's eyes were still shut tight. He could

almost feel Grastow's hot breath on his neck. But the slight tingling told him that he had been transported. He opened his eyes to find himself in the pod room on deck 31. He was alone.

Wesley took some dust-free cloth from a box. He held it over his mouth and nose. He didn't want to set off alarms just by breathing into the air.

The sound of the door opening sent him hurrying behind a pod. He ducked down.

A white-suited figure entered. From the size and shape, Wesley knew it was Emil Costa. The boy remembered the phaser that the scientist carried. He ducked down farther.

The door opened again. It was a stocky figure in another white suit. The new visitor took off his helmet. He wiped a hand over his thick eyebrows.

"Go ahead, take your helmet off," said Karn Milu to the old man. "There's no one around to see us."

With shaking hands, Emil Costa took off his helmet. He stared at pod one. "Did you kill her?"

Karn Milu laughed. "Don't be silly," he said. "It was an accident. In her state of mind, something was bound to happen."

"She didn't want me to tell you about the microbe," said Emil. "She knew it was wrong."

"But she agreed," Milu reminded him. "You both did. You can't keep your findings a secret. You have discovered a germ so small that it cannot be filtered out by any biofilter. Imagine how that germ could be used," exclaimed Dr. Milu, "especially for weapons!"

The Betazoid's voice became friendly now. "Emil, in all our years of service to the Federation, we have never asked for much for ourselves. This is our last chance to get rich!"

Emil ran a hand over his short hair. "What good is money?" he said sadly.

"Why, you could live like a king, Emil!"

Emil swallowed. "To whom would you sell it?"

"The Ferengi have already shown interest," answered the Betazoid. "And there are Romulans who would pay a good price."

"I don't know," said Emil, shaking his head.

"You don't have to get your hands dirty," said Milu. "I'll make the deal. Just tell me which planet we were orbiting when you discovered the microbe. If your wife hadn't destroyed the records, I could have found out myself!"

Suddenly Emil stood taller. "I'm glad she did it!" he declared. "Maybe we haven't always been completely honest. But selling out the Federation is something we've never done!"

Karn Milu frowned. "I've risked a lot for this deal. Just tell me the name of that planet."

Wesley was shocked by all he was hearing. He

sucked in his breath. At the same time, he managed to breathe in a piece of the cloth he held over his mouth. He choked.

The two scientists quickly turned. "Who's there?" growled Karn Milu.

Wesley rose to his feet. "Uh, hello," he said. "Don't tell him, Dr. Costa!"

"What are you doing, Wesley?" cried Emil. "I wouldn't have told him."

But Dr. Milu was taking no chances. He moved toward the young ensign and grabbed him by his neck. The Betazoid was very strong. Before Wesley knew what was happening, Karn Milu was dragging him toward pod number one.

"Open the pod!" Milu ordered Emil Costa.

Emil paused for a second. Then he sighed and opened the double-sealed hatch. Head bowed, the old man turned away.

"No!" Wesley screamed. But the stocky Betazoid pinned his arms to his sides. He stuffed him inside the air-tight pod and closed the hatch. Wesley could hear the scientists sealing the pod.

Wesley screamed and pounded on the inside of the pod. But not a sound could be heard outside. With horror, the boy realized they could have killed him immediately by programming the pod to be airless. But they had let him live.

At least until the air ran out.

CHAPTER 6

Lieutenant Worf quickened his step. He neared the cleanrooms on deck 31. He had received a strange message from the transporter operator, O'Brien. Why, Worf wondered, was Wesley Crusher beaming to the pod room?

The Klingon had only a short time left to find a murderer. He did not want to spend it chasing down a teenager. But O'Brien's words, "life and death," crossed his mind.

He stopped at a door. "Worf to enter," he barked.

"Lieutenant Worf not cleared," the computer replied.

Worf growled. "Security override!"

Now the door opened. Worf moved down the hall between the dark clean rooms. Racks of white suits stood like ghosts along the wall. Worf didn't know why, but a shiver went down his back. He drew his phaser.

He heard the racks of suits rustling. But he was just a second too slow. As he turned he was struck by the phaser beam. It ripped through his body. The wound was low on his leg. The charge did not reach to his brain. Worf fell and tried to roll away.

He got off one wild shot. Then a second beam struck him in the shoulder. His head exploded in a single blast of pain. Then everything went black.

Captain Picard watched his first officer lead the Kreel delegates into the shuttle bay. *The Kreel sure move slowly for such long-legged beings,* thought the captain. The shuttle should have left six minutes ago, and Picard hated to be late.

"Captain!" called Riker. "Let me introduce Admiral Ulree, First Assistant Kwalrak, and the other Kreel delegates."

Picard nodded. "Captain Jean-Luc Picard," he replied. Welcome to the *Enterprise*. This is Commander Data." He pointed to the tall android.

"I'm sorry we have to leave so quickly, but the ceremonies on Kayran Rock will be starting. We can get to know each other on the way."

"Yes, indeed," Kwalrak whispered to Riker.

Rolling his eyes, Riker led the Kreel aboard the shuttlecraft *Ericksen*. Kwalrak took Will's arm and dragged him to the back of the ship. The rest of the Kreel wanted the window seats.

Outside the shuttle the captain was angry. "Now where is Emil Costa?" he asked Data.

"He would seem to be late," the android answered. "But wait!" Data turned his yellow eyes toward the door. "I hear him coming."

Emil Costa hurried into the shuttle bay. He looked a mess. Sweat stood out on his face. "I—I am sorry," he panted. "Some last minute things—"

"Yes, yes, Doctor," muttered Picard. "Take your seat."

Emil Costa quickly boarded the shuttle. He sank into a seat without looking at the others.

When all were aboard, the door clanked shut. "Over here, Data!" called Will Riker. He pushed Kwalrak over and made room for the android.

"If there is too little room here," said Data, I can sit in the cockpit with the pilot."

"No!" Will grabbed Data and pulled the android down between him and the Kreel assistant.

"Thank you," said Data. "I am not used to riding as a passenger. Usually I pilot the craft."

"Well, today you are a guest," insisted Will. "Sit back and act like one!"

The lights in the shuttlecraft dimmed to a soft glow. The ship slid off its pad and sped into space.

Trapped inside the pod, Wesley Crusher was starting to feel dizzy. He knew that the air was growing thin. He tried to breathe evenly. There wasn't anything to do but sit and wait. Either someone would save him or his air would run out.

Wes kept his eyes on the gray glass, watching for someone to appear. But his eyelids felt heavy. It would be so easy to slip off to sleep.

Suddenly a vision in white was looking down through the gray window. Wes blinked in surprise. In a moment the hatch opened. Fresh air poured in.

The figure in white lifted Wesley out of the pod. "Are you in need of medical help?" he asked.

"Not right now," gasped Wesley. "They—those two sealed me in there. Emil Costa—"

The rescuer took off his helmet. The Vulcan face looked closely at Wesley. "Are you all right?" Saduk asked. "Emil Costa is the only reason I am here," he reported. "He asked me to check on an experiment for him. Otherwise, I wouldn't have been in this area."

"We've got to stop them!" cried Wesley.

"One thing at a time, Ensign Crusher," said the Vulcan. "There is a man outside this room who is either dead or badly hurt."

"Who?" exlaimed Wesley.

Saduk pointed toward the door. Wesley hurried out. He saw no dead man, but one very live Klingon. Worf was staring past one of the coat racks toward the floor. As he drew closer, Wesley could see a white boot sticking out from behind the rack.

Lieutenant Worf pointed his tricorder at a plump, white-suited figure lying there. Wesley rushed to get a closer look. He wished he hadn't. The man's chest was burned black.

"No rush to call sickbay," Worf muttered. "This is

the work of a phaser set on full. I was luckier—my attacker had his phaser set to stun."

"You were shot, too!" gasped Wesley. "What is going on here?"

Worf knelt beside the dead man. He pulled off the helmet. They all knew the bushy eyebrows and graying hair.

"Karn Milu!" exclaimed Wesley.

Worf glared at the teenager. "Report, Ensign. What do you know about this?"

Wesley gulped. "He and Emil Costa had an argument. It was about a microbe that the Costas discovered and kept secret. It seems this certain germ cannot be destroyed. Karn Milu wanted to sell it. I was listening, and they caught me and sealed me in a pod. And Emil Costa had a phaser!"

Worf hit his communicator badge. "Security alert! Capture Dr. Emil Costa. He is armed with a phaser and dangerous."

The alert went to every part of the ship. It also went to the shuttlecraft, which was tied into the communication system. Aboard the *Ericksen*, all talk stopped.

"I repeat," came the Klingon's voice. "Capture Emil Costa."

The captain turned to look at Emil. Instead, he got a good look at the business end of a phaser.

"Don't move!" the scientist cried. He waved the

phaser around the cabin. "I'm not going back to the *Enterprise*! I'm not!"

"What is this!" growled Admiral Ulree.

Costa pointed the phaser at the Kreel admiral. A Kreel orderly jumped to his feet. Costa turned and drilled the orderly in the chest with a phaser beam. He fell to the floor of the craft, stunned.

"Don't move!" screamed Emil insanely. "I know how to use this thing!"

"Doctor," Picard said evenly, "you are putting us all in danger. Please put down the phaser."

"No!" cried Emil. "I'm not going back there!" He rushed into the cockpit.

They heard Emil yelling at the pilot. "What are you doing? Don't turn back!" he shouted at her.

"Data," snapped Picard. He knew that the android could stand up to phaser fire better than the rest of them.

But before Data could get to the cockpit, they heard a cry. The shuttlecraft tipped sideways. It was Riker who reached the cockpit first.

He found the pilot, Ensign Hamer, on the floor. Emil Costa was shooting up the shuttle controls with his phaser. Smoke poured from the control panel. Riker grabbed Costa from behind. He easily wrestled the old man to the floor and slapped away the phaser.

But the little shuttle was out of control. It tipped

first to one side, then to the other. Kreel and humans were tossed about the cabin. The lights flashed on and off. The Kreel howled like children.

Data rushed to the helm. He gently moved Ensign Hamer and sat down at the controls.

"Steering is out," Data called to Picard. "Communication systems are dead. The engines are not hurt. In fact, we are picking up speed."

The captain slapped his communicator badge. "Picard to *Enterprise*." There was no answer.

"Out of range," said Data. "The *Enterprise* is moving in the other direction.

"How is Ensign Hamer?" asked Riker.

"She is all right. She was only stunned," answered Data. "But she faces the same danger that we all do."

"Danger?" asked Riker.

"We are headed toward the Kreel asteroid belt," said the android. "We have no way to correct our course or our speed."

Picard and Riker looked out the window. Up ahead, they could see a band of brown objects floating in space. From the distance, they looked like bits of dust. But they all knew those chunks of space litter were larger than the shuttlecraft. A few were larger than the *Enterprise*.

Riker returned to the cabin. The Kreel orderly was sitting up now. The rest of the Kreel were glaring at Emil Costa. "He must be punished,"

Admiral Ulree insisted. "He hurt my officer."

"What is happening?" asked Kwalrak. Her long legs were shaking.

"Nothing," Riker lied. "Data is fixing the controls."

He looked toward the cockpit. He hoped his lie had a bit of truth in it.

The asteroids were getting closer. They no longer looked like dust. They looked exactly like what they were—huge, jagged rocks.

The android reported, "Captain, I believe I can put all energy into the steering system."

"Make it so," ordered Picard.

Data made a few more repairs. "I am ready," the android said. "I may be able to steer her."

"*May* be able?" the captain repeated.

"I cannot be sure until I try."

Data's fingers flew over the control panel. He sent all energy to steering. The craft moved slightly from its course.

But they were now heading right into the asteroid belt. The floating rocks looked huge. It seemed they would certainly crash.

The cabin rang with thuds as small asteroids hit the outer wall. One of the Kreel screamed. Another began a low song. *It is probably a death chant,* thought Picard.

Data shook his head. "This is not working."

Captain Picard's eyes narrowed. "What if we slow to match the speed and course of the asteroids? Couldn't we float safely among them?"

"Yes," Data agreed. "But once we shut down the engines, it is unlikely we could start them again. We would be trapped."

The ship shook as another asteroid hit. They were closing in fast on a giant black one.

"We haven't got much choice," Picard said.

"Yes, sir," answered Data. He reached under the control panel and pulled out some wires. The engines died suddenly. The little ship began to slow. By now, the entire window was filled with the big black asteroid. But they weren't gaining on it anymore. "Well done, Data," said Picard. "See if you can send out some kind of signal for help."

"Yes, Captain. But there is one problem. The more energy we use for a distress signal, the less we have for life support."

Will Riker found himself sitting in the back of the shuttlecraft. Now, however, Kwalrak wasn't bothering him. Wanting to keep away from Emil Costa, she had gone to sit with her fellow Kreel. The scientist sat hunched beside Riker. He looked as miserable as a person could look.

"Why did you do it?" Riker asked.

The old man stared at him. "They would have killed me if I had stayed aboard the *Enterprise*. I couldn't go back, no matter what!"

Riker frowned. "Who would have killed you?"

"The ones who killed Lynn," Emil whispered.

"Who exactly is that?"

Emil shook his head. "I don't know. Karn Milu may have something to do with it. I don't know for sure."

"Karn Milu," repeated Riker. "Why would he harm you?"

"That stupid microbe!" Emil cried. "I wish I had never found it. It cost Lynn her life!"

The ship shook as another asteroid banged against it. They were drifting fairly safely now. But it was only a matter of time before a larger asteroid tore them apart.

Wesley Crusher had just returned to the bridge when the signal came. "Distress signal!" he cried.

"I read it too," reported Worf. "It could be the *Ericksen*." He worked over the controls until a readout came up on his screen. "They are in the Kreel asteroid belt!" he said.

Geordi rose from the captain's chair. He leaned over Worf's shoulder. "They're too far away. We'll have to get closer to transport them. Shields up," he ordered. "La Forge to O'Brien!"

"O'Brien here," answered the transporter operator.

"Lock onto the distress signal," said Geordi. "I want to beam the shuttlecraft to the main bay."

"The shuttle is awfully close to an asteroid," said O'Brien. "It would be safer to lock onto life forms only. Otherwise, we don't know what all we'll bring over."

"Okay," muttered Geordi, "but be quick. When we lower the shields to transport, we could get hit by one of those rocks."

"Aye, sir," answered O'Brien. "Transporter Room Two is standing by to help."

Geordi watched the dark shapes of the asteroids come closer. He heard Deanna Troi beside him. "I sense they are alive," she said. "But in danger."

"We're moving into the asteroid belt," reported Wesley. As he spoke, thuds sounded overhead. The ship shook.

"Shields holding," announced Worf.

"Open all channels," Geordi ordered. "Captain Picard, anyone on the *Ericksen*, do you read me?"

On the shuttlecraft all eyes widened. Geordi's voice sounded over all four Starfleet communicator badges.

"Picard here," answered the captain. "Good to hear your voice, Geordi! We are drifting behind a large asteroid."

As if to make his point, the *Ericksen* was hit soundly. The Kreel wailed loudly.

Data looked out the window. He slapped his communicator. "Geordi, beam us up immediately. We are about to crash."

Data was right. The last hit had sent them straight toward the giant asteroid.

On the bridge Worf ordered, "Shields down!"

"Transporter Room One," snapped Geordi, "beam up eight. Transporter Room Two, wait two seconds, then pick up the other three."

"Energizing," said O'Brien in Room One.

O'Brien couldn't be blamed for locking onto his commanding officers first. Picard, Data, and Riker disappeared from the *Ericksen*. They were quickly followed by Admiral Ulree, Kwalrak, and three other Kreel. Only Ensign Hamer, the wounded Kreel orderly, and Emil Costa were still on the out-of-control shuttle. Ensign Hamer looked at Emil and the Kreel. Her smile seemed to say that they would surely be saved, too.

They were, just seconds later. It was right before the small shuttlecraft crashed into the asteroid. The *Ericksen* exploded into millions of bright bits. Each piece spun off and became a sparkle in the Kreel asteroid belt.

CHAPTER 7

Lieutenant Worf dragged Emil Costa by the arm. They moved down the hall to the security cells.

"I didn't kill anyone!" yelled Emil.

Eyes ahead, Worf growled, "Questioning will begin after you are safely in your cell."

"I know what I did aboard the *Ericksen* was wrong," said Emil. "But I had to get off the *Enterprise*. With two deaths now, can you see why?"

They turned a corner. Worf led the scientist into one of the cells. The Klingon stepped out and pressed a button. Emil sprang toward the open doorway. But he bounced off the invisible force field. He sighed and sat down on the bed.

"I have many questions to ask you," said Worf. "The most important is, did you kill Karn Milu?"

"No," answered the old man. "When I left him, he was alive."

"Did you kill your wife?"

"No!" Emil cried. "Get out of here! Go away!"

He certainly didn't look like a dangerous killer, thought Worf. The small, white-haired man lay curled up on the bed. He shook with sobs. But he was a man charged with terrible crimes. The Kreel wanted to punish him themselves, but the Federation murder charge came first.

"What drove you to it?" asked Worf. "Did Karn Milu tell you that he killed your wife?"

"He probably did kill her," Emil moaned. "But he never told me. And I swear he was alive when I left him. I didn't kill anyone!"

Deanna Troi and Wesley Crusher quietly entered the security room. They stood behind Worf.

"Wesley!" cried Emil. He ran toward the force field and was bounced back again. "Tell the lieutenant that I didn't kill anyone! Tell them you only saw us arguing. I swear I didn't kill anyone!"

"Ensign," warned Worf, "don't say a word. You are a witness."

"Yes, sir." Wesley started for the door.

"Wesley!" shouted the scientist. "I need a lawyer. If you could pick anybody on board, who would it be?"

Wesley answered quickly. "Data."

"Get me Data," the old man told Worf. "I won't answer any more questions without him."

The Klingon tapped his communicator badge. "Worf to Captain Picard."

"Picard here. We are about to leave for Kayran Rock. Even with all that has happened, we have a party to go to. We've decided to beam the Kreel to the asteroid. I want to be sure they arrive safely."

"Understood," said Worf. "I wanted you to know that Dr. Costa has asked that Data act as his lawyer."

"We'll decide this when I return to the ship. I suppose we should ask Data himself. Picard Out."

Worf turned to Emil. "You will stay in your cell until Commander Data returns from Kayran Rock."

Picard, Data, and Riker soon found themselves on the first starbase built inside an asteroid. A pocket had been carved out of the giant rock for Starfleet's use. The walls of the base were cold black rock. The asteroid was really a small planet that had no atmosphere. No blanket of gasses protected it against the coldness of space.

Now the three *Enterprise* crewmen and the Kreel delegates were celebrating in the starbase lounge. Picard had met an old friend and was enjoying a talk. Data was surrounded by a curious crowd. Everyone was always anxious to meet the android and test his amazing memory.

Will Riker was not having such a good time. Unfortunately, dance music was playing. He tried to blend into the black walls, but Kwalrak winked at him from across the room. "Shall we dance?" she called as she shuffled closer.

Kwalrak wrapped her long arms around the commander and moved him onto the dance floor.

But she surprised him. Rather than flirting, she talked politics. "Why don't you give us transporter technology?" the Kreel assistant asked. "You've seen how dangerous shuttle transportation can be."

"We live by the prime directive," answered Will. "We don't interfere in the development of other planets and peoples."

"We could buy transporter technology from the Ferengi!" Kwalrak warned.

Riker shook his head. "Let me tell you what would happen. If you didn't understand the technology yourself, you would be at the mercy of the Ferengi. They would sell you the first units cheaply. Then they could charge you anything for more transporters and repairs. They would end up owning your planet."

Kwalrak moaned. "If the prices they are offering us now are the low ones, I'd hate to see the high ones."

Riker smiled at her. He suddenly noticed that her large brown eyes were quite pretty. "You've developed space travel. You've developed huge weapons systems. Why can't your scientists work on transporter technology?"

Kwalrak nodded. She gave Riker a squeeze. When he pulled away, she laughed. "Don't worry," she whispered. "This is just my way of flirting with you. Ulree would have us both killed if there really were something between us. And Will, if I did want you, you'd have been mine by now."

Somehow, Riker didn't doubt her.

The dance ended. Kwalrak pinched Will's beard and moved away into the crowd.

"Picard to Riker." The captain's voice came over Will's communicator. "Let's say our good-byes and go home."

The doors of the security section slid open. Data strode in. Emil Costa jumped to his feet. He moved close to the force field of his cell.

"Commander Data!" he called. "They were true to their words. They sent you to help me."

Data walked to the edge of the cell. "Why do you wish me to act as your lawyer?"

"On Wesley Crusher's suggestion," said Emil. "I'm in trouble. I know that now. I will admit to every crime I ever committed, going back to the biofilter days. But I did not murder anyone!"

"You say you did not murder Karn Milu, no matter how it looks?" asked Data.

"Yes!" barked the old man. "I didn't do it! I did not kill Lynn or Dr. Milu!"

"If you did not," asked Data, "who did?"

"I don't know," screamed Emil. "I thought Karn Milu killed my wife. But now he is dead. I don't know who it is!"

"Calm yourself, Doctor," said Data. "I will plead your case. But I can't say you will win. Many people feel sure that you are the murderer."

"What have I got to lose?" whispered Emil. "I've already lost everything."

Data nodded. Emil Costa's future did not look good. If he was cleared of the murder charge, he would still face a Kreel court. "I will act as your lawyer only at the trial for the murder of Karn Milu," explained the android. "If you need a lawyer after that, you will have to look somewhere else."

"Understood," nodded Emil. "By the way, Commander, thank you for saving us on the shuttlecraft. I am truly sorry for what I did. For my madness on the shuttle, I will accept any punishment—but not for things I did not do."

Captain Picard stepped up to the transporter pad. He held out his hand to the small woman who had just appeared there.

"Judge Watanabe! Welcome aboard the *Enterprise*. Come right this way."

Jean-Luc Picard and Judge Ishe Watanabe rode the turbolift to the bridge. They went straight to the meeting room. Commander Riker, Lieutenant Commander Data, and Lieutenant Worf jumped to their feet as the two entered the room. Picard quickly introduced the judge who would be hearing Emil Costa's case.

"Thank you for setting this meeting," said Judge Watanabe. "We could have talked by communicator, but I prefer a face-to-face meeting."

The judge was a small, quiet-looking woman. But her firm voice called for respect. "Now, who will be acting as Dr. Costa's lawyer?"

Picard sat forward. "Emil Costa has already asked Commander Data to be his lawyer."

"Very good," said the judge.

Worf was moving about in his seat. "Lieutenant Worf, do you wish to say something?" asked Picard.

The Klingon sat up stiffly. "I would like to act as prosecuting attorney," he said. "I know the facts of the case already."

"I have no problem with that," said Judge Watanabe. "This is your ship. The case should be settled by those within it."

Then the tiny judge slapped her hands on the table and rose. "At ten o'clock tomorrow morning," she declared, "report to Starbase Meeting Room B. Emil Costa must appear. We'll arrange sleeping quarters on Kayran Rock for everyone."

"For Dr. Costa," added Worf, "make them high security. We will only beam him cell-to-cell."

Picard and Riker led the judge back to the transporter room. Data and Worf were left alone.

"I plan to see this murderer put away for a long

time," warned Worf. "Data, are you forgetting what he did to you on the shuttlecraft?"

"Yes," answered Data. "I am forgetting that."

Worf shrugged. He marched toward the doorway. "I will see you in court."

Wesley Crusher rose from his desk. "I'm trying to write it all down, Deanna," he said. "I want to be sure I remember everything I saw or heard before Karn Milu's murder."

"Worf and I appreciate what you've done. It's too bad we were too late to help Dr. Milu," Deanna Troi replied.

A voice at the door boomed, "This is Lieutenant Worf. May I enter?"

"Come in," called Wesley.

Worf nodded to Wesley and Deanna. "Since you are together, I will bring you up to date. The trial begins at ten o'clock tomorrow morning at the starbase. Ensign Crusher," Worf said, "I would like you to beam there with me tonight. Emil Costa is also beaming to a cell on the asteroid. I will act as prosecuting attorney in the case," he added.

"Excellent!" exclaimed Wesley.

"And Data will be acting as defense attorney," he explained.

"Wow!" said Wesley, a bit nervously. "He's going to cross-examine me!"

Worf nodded. "Pack enough uniforms for a few days," he said. "I'll be back in an hour."

"I should be going, too," said Deanna. She smiled at Wesley and followed the lieutenant out.

"I feel good about this case," said Worf. He walked quickly down the hall. Deanna hurried to keep up. "Crusher will make it clear that the doctor had a phaser when he went to meet Karn Milu. Emil had a reason to kill and a chance to do it. In fact, he had a few reasons. He was greedy. He was being blackmailed. He wanted revenge. Costa believed that Karn Milu had killed his wife! And I have another witness who heard Karn Milu threaten to kill Lynn Costa."

Deanna's eyes opened wide in surprise. "Is there anything else I can do?" she asked.

"I need you to go through Karn Milu's personal files and records. I will be at the trial, but Captain Picard will remain on board the *Enterprise*. Let him know if you find anything helpful."

Deanna's forehead wrinkled. "Is there any way it could be somebody else?" she asked.

Worf looked at her. "Counselor, we need to back up our case, not come up with new ideas."

"Understood," answered Deanna. "I'll check out Karn Milu's files and report later."

CHAPTER 8

Deanna Troi rubbed her eyes. She thought about going to her quarters for some rest. *Better start on Karn Milu's records*, she told herself. She took the turbolift to the science offices on deck 5.

The halls were empty. Not many of the scientists felt like working. The head of the department was dead, and the most famous scientist on board had been charged with the murder.

As Deanna rounded a corner, she bumped into a figure hurrying from the other direction. Shana Russel jumped back.

"I just heard!" the young woman gasped. "This is horrible! How can he be dead?"

"It's been a shock," Deanna agreed. "Are you coming from Dr. Milu's office? Why were you there?"

"I don't know!" cried Shana. "Oh, what is happening to us?"

Deanna put her arm around the girl. "You must be brave," she said. "Emil Costa is standing trial for Dr. Milu's murder. You will probably be called for questioning."

Shana shook her head. "I don't know anything! What will I tell them?" The young woman leaned on the wall. "This is not how I imagined it would be. The Costas, the *Enterprise*—I thought I was the luckiest kid in my class. But now it's all over."

Deanna patted Shana's arm. "You're still on the *Enterprise*. And you still have work to do."

The girl smiled a little. "Thank you for being so understanding, Counselor Troi."

"It's my job," Deanna said. Then she continued down the hall. She wondered if Karn Milu's door would be locked. If it was, she had only to contact Worf. He would give her a security override.

Deanna also wondered how much information she would need to read through. Betazoids always kept so many records.

Deanna Troi had looked up to Dr. Milu. She hoped she wouldn't find signs of more wrongdoings. Whatever she found, Deanna told herself, would help Worf get at the truth. That's what really mattered.

Milu's door whooshed open as she neared. It was unlocked. Deanna entered the office and stared at the cases of insects. Then her eyes went to the desk. She stopped. The computer screen was on!

Perhaps the scientist had left it that way, thought Deanna. But Karn Milu was not the careless type. Had somebody else been in his office?

The computer was already opened to Karn Milu's files. Deanna worked long into the night. She read the files and listened to tapes of his logs. Everything was very businesslike. This information was meant for the public, Deanna decided. Where were happy birthday messages, to-do lists, bits of favorite poems? Where were his personal thoughts?

She stood and looked about the room. It was quite usual for a Betazoid to keep a secret diary or notebook. But it wasn't an easy office to search. The place was, in fact, crawling with bugs.

Deanna was surprised when the door slid open. She turned to greet the visitor. But no one entered. She moved toward the open door, calling, "Is anybody there?"

In answer came quick footsteps. But when she reached the hall, whoever had been there was gone.

Someone must have come to the office expecting to find it empty. Deanna had surprised the visitor. This did not look good. Counting herself and Shana Russel, the unseen caller was the third visitor to Milu's office that night.

She touched her badge. "Troi to Worf."

"Worf here."

"Sorry to bother you," she said. "But I'm in Karn Milu's office. I feel we should seal it off. I think people have been coming in and out of here."

"Right away," said Worf. "But I'm on Kayran Rock. Can you wait until a security team arrives?"

"Yes," breathed Deanna. But she felt uneasy.

The Betazoid crossed her arms and stood in the doorway of the office. She didn't know why she felt frightened. But it seemed like somebody was out there, just out of sight, watching her.

She heard a noise. Footsteps. She moved back into the office. The footsteps kept coming. It sounded like just one person. It was certainly not the security team that Worf had promised.

The footsteps stopped. She wanted to scream. What was he waiting for?

A large figure rounded the corner. Deanna gasped.

Then a smile lit up her face. She rushed to meet the bearded first officer.

Riker smiled at the hug she gave him. "Hello," he laughed. "To what do I owe this warm welcome?"

"Silly fear," she replied. "I've been here by myself, going through Karn Milu's records. I must be getting jumpy."

"Worf told me you had some strange visitors," said Riker. "The security team will be here any second, but I was close by." Riker's voice dropped to a whisper. "While we're alone," he said, "I have something to tell you. I've put in for shore leave. This thing between Lynn and Emil got me thinking, you know, about two people needing to be alone together. Why don't we try it?"

"That's sweet of you," she smiled.

Just then, four security men noisily rounded the corner. "Security team here," said the leader.

"Right on time," Will replied. He bowed to Deanna. "About that other matter, think about it."

"I will, Commander," she promised.

Deanna Troi rubbed her forehead. Hours had passed. Still she had found nothing of interest in Karn Milu's files. She was about ready to give up when a security officer peeked in the doorway.

"Commander La Forge wishes to enter," he said.

Deanna rose from Milu's desk. "Geordi," she sighed, "thanks for coming. I thought maybe you could help me."

"What can I do?" Geordi asked.

The Betazoid waved her hand around the office. "I have reason to believe," she explained, "that something is hidden here. But I've looked everywhere. I thought, with your special vision—"

"Say no more," said Geordi. He moved slowly around the office. He was blind, but his VISOR took the place of eyes. He could sense things by the wave lengths they put out.

Geordi stopped before a dark wood case that

held some dead insects. He moved one of the bugs. It fell to dust in his fingers. But underneath it, pinned to the board, was a computer chip.

"Bingo!" he cried.

The counselor let out her breath. "Thank you, Geordi!" she exclaimed. "Let's see what's on it."

Geordi put the chip into a slot on Karn Milu's computer. Deanna's fingers ran over the keyboard. A jumble of words and letters appeared on the screen. They made no sense at all.

"It's a code," declared Deanna.

"Then the computer can read it," Geordi said.

"You don't understand." Deanna shook her head. "It's Betazoid. It is based on thought patterns deep within the mind. Karn Milu did not consciously know the code when he wrote it."

"What?" Geordi looked confused.

"He wrote it while in a trance. He knew that he could read it sometime in the future if he thought hard enough."

"I'll bet Data could—" Geordi began.

"Only the person who writes it can read it. There is no code more secret."

"Can you go into that kind of trance?" asked Geordi.

Deanna shook her head. "I'm not even full Betazoid."

Geordi put a hand on her shoulder. "You don't know what you can do until you try. Give it a go."

"Of course I'll try," the counselor promised. She pulled the chip from its slot and held it. "Something has been hidden from us the whole time. I feel it. Perhaps this is it."

"Call me if you need help," offered Geordi.

Deanna sighed. "Unless I get some sleep, I won't be able to read my own name. Thanks, Geordi. I will probably call you again in a few hours."

Judge Ishe Watanabe banged her gavel. "Let the record show," she announced, "that Emil Costa has pleaded innocent to the murder of Karn Milu. The court will now hear opening arguments."

Worf rose to his full height. "Karn Milu was murdered aboard the *Enterprise*," began the Klingon. "He was killed by a phaser set to full. As our witness will report, the killing happened seconds after an argument between Karn Milu and Emil Costa. The witness will swear that Emil Costa went to see Karn Milu armed with a phaser. Indeed, Dr. Costa later used that same phaser to try to hijack a shuttlecraft.

"Emil Costa had reason to murder," Worf continued. "He believed that Karn Milu had killed his wife. He was also being pressed to turn over a secret discovery. Against Starfleet rules, the Costas, together with Karn Milu, were planning to sell a discovery made aboard the *Enterprise* to non-Federation parties."

Worf folded his big arms. "I believe," he rumbled, "that you will find Emil Costa guilty of the murder of Karn Milu."

Worf sat down. All eyes in the courtroom turned to Commander Data. The android stood.

"Your Honor," he said with a bow, "Emil Costa pleads innocent to the charge of murder. Yes, he did have reason to argue with Karn Milu. But there is not enough proof to convict him of the murder. The whole case rests on one overheard conversation. There is no witness to the murder itself. No one saw Emil Costa point the phaser at Karn Milu.

"Dr. Costa admits to past wrongs," Data told the quiet courtroom. "But you will have to decide whether one overheard conversation proves a man is a murderer."

The screen of the video machine faded to black. The court had just watched Wesley Crusher's taped account of his visit to deck 31. Worf turned to the young ensign in the witness chair. "Now that the court has seen this statement, do you wish to change anything?" he asked.

"No, sir," answered Wes. "But I might add a few things."

"Such as?"

"Well," said the teenager, "I haven't really

described how scared Emil Costa was—both before his wife's funeral and after. When he grabbed that phaser out of his drawer, I really had the feeling it was for protection."

"Would you describe Emil Costa as upset during his meeting with Karn Milu?"

"Yes."

"And are you certain you heard Emil Costa accuse Karn Milu of killing his wife?"

The teenager nodded. "He said that, yes. But Dr. Milu said that her death was an accident. All he wanted to talk about was the secret microbe."

"Would you say the men were both angry?"

"Yes," Wesley answered.

Worf nodded. "After you were rescued from the pod, you saw Karn Milu's body. What were your first thoughts?"

Wesley tried not to look at Emil Costa. "I thought Dr. Costa had killed him," he whispered.

"Could you say that louder?" asked Worf.

"I thought Dr. Costa had killed him!" Wes said too loudly. He sank back into his chair.

Worf nodded firmly. He turned to the judge. "I have no more questions at this time. I may want to call this witness again later."

"Commander Data," said Judge Watanabe, "you may cross-examine."

Data walked to the stand. "Good day, Ensign Crusher," he said. "The last time you saw Karn Milu and Emil Costa, they were working together to close you in a pod. Is that true?"

"That's right," Wesley said nervously.

"They were not arguing?" Data went on.

"No," answered Wes. "But they could have started up again."

"Why would they?" asked Data. "Emil Costa was about to get what he wanted. He was about to leave the ship. In a few minutes, he would be rid of Karn Milu forever. Why would he kill Karn Milu?"

Worf jumped up. "I object! The witness cannot know what another person was thinking!"

"Overruled," said the judge. "The ensign's view of what happened is all we have." She turned to the nervous young man. "Do you have an answer?"

"I think I do," Wesley said. "Emil also had the idea that Karn Milu killed his wife."

"Isn't it true," Data insisted, "that Karn Milu told Emil that Lynn's death was an accident?"

"Yes."

"Can you say Emil Costa was absolutely sure that his wife was murdered?"

"No," muttered the teenager. "Like all of us, he wasn't sure what exactly happened to her."

Data's golden eyes never left the young man. "Ensign," he said softly, "Emil Costa has been your teacher and friend. Is that not true?"

"It's true," Wes answered.

"Do you think he is capable of murder?"

Wesley's mouth opened, but at first no words came out. He shook his head. "No," he gasped. "I can't believe he did it."

Worf's stiff back slumped just a little.

"Vagra II," said Emil Costa. "That's the planet where I found the microbe."

Judge Watanabe had just put Dr. Costa on the stand. She appeared anxious to get at the truth.

The judge leaned toward Emil Costa. "When did you decide to keep your discovery a secret?"

The old scientist wiggled in his seat. "I knew it was special right away. I tested it on Lynn's newest filters. This little microbe could not be beaten. Lynn and I moved the information to our private file. We wanted to control the discovery until we had a clear idea of what to do with it. Thoughts of its uses in weapons were frightening."

Emil took a drink of water. He leaned forward. "I launched the only sample into space. Only Lynn and I knew where to get more. Then we made our first mistake. We went to Karn Milu. He said we should secretly sell our findings to whoever would pay the most. Milu offered to set up the sale for a twenty-five percent cut. We agreed. But we didn't give him any information.

"But Lynn got scared. Without telling me, she erased every record of the microbe. Milu was mad.

He wanted the secret! He began to threaten Lynn. By this time, I agreed with my wife. I wanted nothing more than to forget about the whole thing.

"That was not to be," Emil went on. "Lynn knew we were in danger. I never took her seriously—until her death. Now I know how right she was. It was a terrible thing we did, and we've paid for it—" Emil's words ended in a sob.

Judge Watanabe leaned toward him. "Would you like a rest, Dr. Costa?" she asked.

He shook his head and tried to calm himself.

The judge nodded. "If you are able, I have a few more questions. Dr. Costa, is it usual for scientists to carry phasers?"

"No," Emil replied.

"Then where did you get the weapon?"

The scientist hung his head. "I made it. I was working with a group of science students who were studying phaser technology. I know it's another crime. But Lynn was scared! She wanted some sort of protection. I made two of them."

"Where is the other one?" asked Worf, rising. He was angry that security had allowed such a thing to happen on his ship.

"I don't know," Emil said. "Lynn left it somewhere, or it was stolen. I don't remember."

The old man lifted his head. "But I never fired a phaser until I was on that shuttlecraft. I swear it!

I've done some bad things," cried the scientist, "but not murder. I never killed anyone."

"Who did?" asked the judge.

Emil folded his hands. He shook his head. "I don't know," he swallowed, but they must still be aboard the *Enterprise*."

CHAPTER 9

In her dark room, Deanna Troi slept uneasily. She dreamed of Karn Milu. His face, his voice, his thoughts, and his coded writings filled her mind. He seemed to be trying to tell her his secrets.

At last Deanna gave up on sleep. She slid out of bed and splashed water on her face. She went to her food slot and pushed the machine's wake-up button. "Small pot of English tea," she ordered.

Several seconds passed. Nothing happened. Deanna hit the button again. "Computer," she asked, "may I please have a glass of water?"

Nothing happened. The machine was dead. Deanna didn't have time to worry about a broken food slot. If she wanted something to drink, she would go out and get it. Maybe she could find Geordi. Perhaps he could help her break the code with the computer.

She pulled on her jumpsuit and touched her communicator badge. "Troi to La Forge," she called. "Geordi, can you help me run Karn Milu's code through the computer?"

"Sure," came the answer. "I'll meet you in Engineering."

Deanna grabbed Karn Milu's secret computer chip and hurried out of the cabin. The broken food slot was forgotten.

⚛ ⚛ ⚛

"Geordi," said Deanna. She leaned over La Forge's shoulder. "How long will this take?"

The chief engineer looked closely at the computer screen. "Computer?" he asked. "What's happening with this code?"

"It does not match any system of numbers, letters, or words. It appears to be senseless."

Geordi looked at Deanna and smiled. "Computers always were lousy mind readers."

Deanna patted Geordi's back. "It was a good try. I can't say I'm surprised. It's like a poem that makes no sense."

Suddenly Deanna had an idea. She didn't know if it would work, but she wanted to walk in a holodeck setting and try to remember some Betazoid poetry.

"Thank you Geordi," she said, rushing toward the door.

"You're welcome!" he called after her.

As Deanna reached the turbolift, a voice sounded over her badge. "Security officer to Counselor Troi."

She tapped the badge. "Troi here."

"A service person wants to enter your room to fix your food slot."

"My food slot?" She suddenly remembered the broken machine. "Please let him in. And thank him for being so quick about it."

"The repairs can wait until you are present."

"No need," answered Deanna. "I may not return to my room for hours. Out." Thinking about poetry, she told the turbolift to go to deck 11.

Dr. Grastow moved about, but he could not fit comfortably into the witness chair. Lieutenant Worf walked back and forth in front of him.

"How would you describe your relationship with Dr. Costa?" Worf asked the big Antarean.

Grastow looked warmly at the old man. "I love him," he said. "I live only to serve him."

"Did you hide Dr. Costa in your cabin after his wife's funeral?"

"Yes," answered Grastow. "It was his wish."

"Did you later use force to hold Ensign Crusher in your cabin against his will?"

The Antarean nodded. "I know it was wrong. But

Emil wanted to be alone. I was the only person he trusted."

"What power," Worf growled, "does he hold over you?"

"He and Lynn saved my planet," Grastow answered. "My parents would be dead, my world would be dead, if not for the Costas. I know," cried Grastow, "that Emil couldn't hurt anybody!"

The Klingon stopped walking. "Did you see Emil Costa arm himself with a phaser?"

Grastow looked down at his big hands. "Yes, I did," he whispered.

"Why did he think he needed it?" asked Worf.

"He didn't say." said Gastrow.

"Emil Costa was going to meet a man with whom he had worked for many years. Didn't you think it was strange that he was carrying a phaser?"

"Yes," gulped Grastow. "But he was upset."

"How much did you know about the secret dealings between Karn Milu and Emil Costa?"

"I knew nothing!" cried the big man.

"No further questions," said Worf.

Judge Watanabe turned to Data. "You may question the witness."

The android stood. "Good day, Dr. Grastow."

"Good day," Grastow answered.

"Dr. Grastow, you said that you are so loyal to Dr. Costa that you would do anything for him."

"Yes," Grastow answered. He sounded confused.

"Does 'anything' include murder?"

"I object!" barked Worf. "The witness is not on trial here."

"I only wish to show," said Data, "that others may have had a reason to kill Karn Milu."

"Objection overruled," Judge Watanabe answered. "Let the witness answer."

But Emil Costa had jumped to his feet. He was shouting at his own lawyer. "Grastow didn't do anything. He wasn't there!" The old man was so upset that he tripped over his chair. He would have fallen if Worf had not caught him. The Klingon helped the old scientist sit down again.

Emil looked at Worf gratefully. "Thank you," he said.

Judge Watanabe took off her glasses. "It is getting late," she said. "We will take a break. We'll meet again at ten o'clock tomorrow. Dr. Grastow, you may step down for now."

Everyone began to rise from their chairs. Emil Costa suddenly grabbed Worf's brown hand. "I didn't kill him," he breathed. "My life is over. I have nothing to gain by lying. Find his murderer! You must keep looking!"

Worf stepped back. Shaking his head, he let the security officers lead the scientist away. He didn't know just why, but he was going to do what the old man asked. He was going to keep looking.

It was one of those cloudy days with a good breeze. It was the kind of day Deanna remembered from long ago. The meadow was filled with orange flowers. Moss was soft and green under her boots. A gentle rain hit her face. She felt like a child again. Her mind was clear and open.

Deanna walked along thinking how wonderfully real the holodeck setting appeared. Karn Milu had probably walked in a Betazoid meadow just like this one. If she knew how Milu was feeling, she told herself, she could read the meaning in his words. She didn't have to figure out every letter, just the parts about the Costas and their project.

One word, one name, might lead to others. Lynn, she thought. She would look for Lynn Costa's name.

Deanna turned round and round. She sang silly words from a children's song she remembered. Then she shouted to the wind, "End program!" In a moment, she was in a plain, black room again.

Shaking the rain from her hair, Deanna walked back to her quarters. She felt fresh and awake now. Before entering, she stopped a moment. She sent a thought message to Karn Milu, asking him to help her. It was silly, she knew. But feelings and thoughts could remain after a person was gone.

Deanna entered her quarters. She sat down at the computer screen. She plugged in the chip and went right to work.

The strange code filled the screen. She stared, waiting for something—anything—to jump out at her. She kept a picture of Lynn Costa in her mind. Lynn's name would appear somewhere in the code. She just knew it.

For two hours, the Betazoid kept at it. She never stopped believing in her own powers. She tried to chant the nonsense words, to sing them. All the while, the only picture in her mind was Lynn Costa. *How did Karn Milu feel about her?* Deanna thought.

"A hag," he called her. She blinked. She read it right there in front of her on the screen.

Suddenly small bits began to make sense. Names jumped out at her.

"Queen hag," it said. "Lynn is the queen hag. Emil is a naughty jester. Saduk is the next in line. Grastow is a footman. Shana is jasmine."

She stared at the words. *What did names like footman, jasmine, and jester mean?* she said to herself.

The counselor sat back. Deanna wanted to show this to someone. She touched her communicator. "Troi to Worf."

Worf was in his quarters on the asteroid. He was holding the blue bottle that Deanna found at the murder scene. He remembered how it had been quickly linked to Emil Costa. Had the bottle been planted there to point them in Emil's direction?

The sound on the communicator broke into his thoughts. "Worf here," he snarled. "I must talk to you, Counselor."

"And I need to talk to you," Deanna replied. "We've found a computer chip hidden in Karn Milu's office. It holds coded notes. I've been able to read some of them."

"I'm returning to the ship," said Worf, "Where are you?"

"In my quarters," said the Betazoid. "I'll see you there. Out."

As Lieutenant Worf charged toward his door, Deanna Troi stood slowly. She stretched her back and neck. She remembered the many times Karn Milu had told her to work on her Betazoid powers. He would be proud of her, she felt.

Tea, thought the Betazoid. She turned toward the food slot. She saw a slight trail of steam coming from the slot. *Darn,* she said to herself. *I thought they fixed that thing.*

Deanna took just one step. Then her mind lost control of her legs. She fell forward, gasping. Luckily, she fell on the rug. Her mind stayed with her for the seconds she needed to touch her badge and shout, "Troi to sickbay! Emergency! Emerg—"

Her voice trailed off. The Betazoid's lungs stopped breathing. Her heart stopped beating.

CHAPTER 10

Worf went to the starbase transporter room. He was surprised to find Data there. "You are returning to the *Enterprise*?" Worf asked him.

"Yes," replied Data. "I would like to get back to the ship for a while. It troubles me to think that the real murderer may be at large."

Worf frowned. "You aren't the only one."

"Lieutenant Worf." The voice of Dr. Beverly Crusher came over Worf's communicator badge. "Report to sickbay right away."

"On my way, Doctor," the Klingon answered. "What happened?"

"Deanna Troi," she began, "has had a close brush with death. I want her to rest. But she insists on seeing you."

Worf charged to the transformer platform. Data was not far behind him.

Worf and Data were at the doors of sickbay within moments. Dr. Crusher stood in front of them, her arms crossed. "Deanna has had a close call. I want her to sleep, but she says she must see Worf. Data, will you please go to the bridge and let Captain Picard and Commander Riker know what has happened. I'll give them a full report later."

"Yes, Doctor," the android nodded. He hurried off to the bridge.

"What happened to her?" asked Worf with alarm.

Beverly frowned. "I'm not really sure. When she came in here, she wasn't breathing. Something caused her brain to shut down. We shocked her back to life. When she's stronger, we'll run tests. I expect to find traces of poison."

"Who brought her in?"

"She called sickbay herself. The computer noted the emergency and beamed her directly here. Otherwise," said Beverly, "Deanna would be dead."

The Klingon growled low in his throat. He followed Beverly Crusher into sickbay.

Deanna lay on a bed, her face unusually white. As Worf entered, she smiled weakly.

"Two minutes," warned Beverly Crusher. She shut the door behind her.

Worf knelt by the bed. "I am sorry I put you in danger," he said.

"We're getting close, Worf," Deanna whispered. The real murderer is scared. In my quarters," she breathed, "get the chip. But be careful. There may still be gas in there. See what Karn Milu meant by the "queen hag" entry."

"What?" Worf asked.

"It may be nothing," sighed the Betazoid. She tried to gather enough strength to go on. "In his secret records, Karn Milu wrote: 'Lynn is the queen hag, Emil is a naughty jester, Saduk is next in line, Grastow is a footman, and Shana is jasmine.'"

"Rest," Worf said, patting her hand. He stood and touched his communicator. "Worf to La Forge."

"La Forge here," said the chief engineer.

"Meet me in Deanna Troi's quarters. And bring two tricorders. Out," snapped Worf. He turned back to tell Deanna good-bye. She was already asleep.

△ △ △

Worf rode the turbolift to the deck where the bridge officers lived. Geordi La Forge came off a lift on the other side of the hall. He tossed a tricorder to Worf. Together they walked to Deanna's cabin. "What are we looking for?" Geordi asked.

The Klingon's eyes never left his tricorder display. "A gas that can kill someone in seconds."

"I'm picking up some strange readings," said Geordi. "But nothing strong enough to be dangerous." They stepped into Deanna's room. "Someone was nice enough to air it out for us."

"Niceness has nothing to do with it," growled Worf.

Geordi went to Deanna's food slot. It had been blasted apart with a phaser. He stared at the black hole and the burned wires. "Direct shot!" he said.

Worf was looking at Deanna's desk. The computer screen was off. The chip slots were empty.

"The chip is gone!" he growled. "After Deanna passed out, somebody came in here to steal the chip." Worf turned to the burned food slot. "When they didn't find her body, they decided to destroy clues of their attempted murder. I'm going to Milu's office. Maybe he left other records."

Geordi stopped Worf. "I know you've got a lot on your mind," he called, "but I finished that speedup of the turbolifts you asked for. If you want to go fifteen-percent faster, just say 'speed test.' You will get a fast trip to Engineering."

"Thank you," nodded Worf.

Geordi called to him again. "Do it when you first get on," he warned. "If you do it when the lift is moving, you'll get the ride of your life!"

Worf hardly heard the engineer's last words as he marched away from Deanna's cabin. He'd been wrong about Emil Costa, he told himself. But who else could be the murderer?

Deanna Troi had found something. While he played courtroom on Kayran Rock, Deanna Troi was on the trail of the real murderer. She had needed his help, and he hadn't been there for her!

"Deck five," Worf growled to the turbolift.

A moment later the Klingon stepped out on an empty hall lined with dark offices. The science branch had nearly shut down. He headed for Karn Milu's office, not sure what he would find there.

A security team still guarded the office door. Worf was surprised to find Saduk talking to them.

"Lieutenant Worf," nodded the Vulcan. "I was hoping to go into Dr. Milu's office."

"May I ask why?" asked the lieutenant.

"I thought," said the Vulcan, "that Dr. Milu may have left word about the Microcontamination Project. We don't know who will head the project now."

"Go on in," said Worf. He followed Saduk into the office. The Vulcan sat down in the dead Betazoid's chair. He turned on the computer screen.

After a few minutes, Saduk looked up. "Nothing of use," he declared. "I believe it will be up to the captain to choose a new project leader."

"Lynn is the queen hag," Worf said aloud. "Emil is a naughty jester, Saduk is next in line, Grastow is a footman, and Shana is jasmine."

Saduk blinked. "That is interesting," he said. "Are those your thoughts about us?"

"No," Worf replied. "They're Karn Milu's. Do they mean anything to you?"

"Each one," answered Saduk, "has some meaning. Lynn could certainly be thought of as the queen. I, however, did not think she was hard to get along with. Emil liked a joke. He laughed more than the rest of us. One could say he had been naughty. I was likely to be next in line to head the project. As I understand, the word 'footman' could mean a servant. Do you think Grastow acted as Dr. Costa's servant? As for Shana being 'Jasmine,' I did hear Dr. Milu call her that once."

"Wait," Worf said. "Is Jasmine a name?"

"Karn used it as such," replied Saduk. "I only heard him call her that once."

The Klingon looked over the Vulcan's shoulder. "Look up Shana Russel's file," he ordered. "See what data Karn Milu kept on her."

Saduk tapped the keyboard. They both looked at the screen in surprise. Shana Russel's records only went back to the day she arrived on the *Enterprise*.

"Computer," said Worf, "what about Shana Russel's past?"

"Data removed by order of Karn Milu," replied the computer. "Starbase can supply information."

"How long will that take?"

"Six-point-seven minutes."

"Send it to my command post," barked Worf. As he headed for the door, he looked back at Saduk. "Thank you. And I think you should get the job as head of the project. I will tell the captain as much."

The Vulcan nodded. His face stayed as calm as ever.

Worf stepped into his command room. He went to his food slot for some water. Thinking of Deanna, he held his breath until the glass appeared.

The computer's female voice broke into his thoughts. "Report from starbase," she announced. "Do you wish data by screen or aloud?"

"Aloud," Worf replied.

"Shana Russel," said the computer. "Born Jasmine Terry on Earth, city of Calcutta. Age, twenty-five. Earned science degree—"

"Wait," said Worf. "When did she change her name?"

"Eight-point-five months ago."

"Jasmine Terry." He said the name slowly. He knew where he had heard the first name. But where had he heard that last name before? "Match the name Terry," he ordered, "with names in the records on Lynn and Emil Costa."

"Searching," replied the computer. "One match found. Megan Terry worked with the Costas on the biofilter project twenty-six years ago. She sued the Costas, charging them with stealing biofilter number 8975-G. She said it was her discovery, not theirs. That biofilter became the model used throughout the Federation.

Megan Terry lost her case and any claim to the filter."

"Match Megan Terry and Jasmine Terry," asked Worf.

"Mother and daughter," answered the computer.

"That's enough of that," declared a voice behind him. "Put up your hands."

Worf turned his head enough to see Shana Russel. She was dressed in dark clothes and had a phaser pointed at his head.

"I should have set the phaser on full," she said, "when I shot you before."

"Why didn't you?" Worf raised his hands.

The blond woman grinned. "I liked you. Even I make mistakes. Now back away from that computer."

Worf did as he was told. He'd faced creatures from all over the galaxy. But few of them seemed as cold-hearted as Shana Russel/Jasmine Terry.

"Your mother," he said, "was the one who really discovered the biofilter?"

Shana's pretty face darkened with anger. "It was worse than that! Emil said he was in love with my mother. He promised to leave his wife if she would turn over her work to him. Like a fool, she believed him. The Costas stole her work. They had her moved to another project, and they became famous. Emil refused to accept me at all."

"He knew you?" asked Worf.

"Not really." Her eyes flashed with hate. "He never admitted to being my father, but he is."

The Klingon stood still. He could see that the tiny blond had gone completely mad. She had been raised to seek revenge.

"You have done what you set out to do," Worf said. "You have destroyed them."

Shana smiled. "I know. Killing Lynn was good. But watching Emil suffer was even better. He had no idea who I was, or what was happening to him."

"But Karn Milu knew who you were."

"Of course," she answered. "He knew my mother. After that microbe discovery, Karn wanted someone to spy on the Costas. He came to my school to find me. We changed my name. He taught me Betazoid mind control to fool Deanna Troi." The girl smiled. "I've always been a good student."

"Why did you kill Karn Milu?" Worf asked.

"He was the only one who knew who I was. Plus, it made matters worse for Emil."

"And Deanna Troi?"

"If anyone could catch me," answered the killer, "it would be Counselor Troi." She shook her head. "It's too bad. If she had died as planned, you wouldn't have known about the computer chip. We wouldn't be having this talk."

The young woman pressed a button on Worf's

desk. The door slid open on the empty hall. She waved the phaser. "I'll follow you to the turbolift. One wrong move and I'll cut you in two."

Worf stepped into the hall. "Where are we going?"

"To get a shuttlecraft. My time on the *Enterprise* is over, and so is yours."

Worf walked toward the turbolift. He could feel the phaser behind his back. He moved to the back of the lift. "Deck four," he said.

They began to move. Shana leaned comfortably against the side of the lift. "You're taking this well," she said. "Maybe you will think about staying with me."

"Speed test!" Worf suddenly ordered.

He had time to brace himself, but Shana did not. The sudden speedup made it feel like the floor had dropped out. Shana crashed into the roof, screaming. Then she bounced along the wall. Worf rolled into a curl. He was thrown about, but with less harm. The turbolift whizzed through the ship.

Shana tried to hold on to the phaser. But the Klingon made the fight short. He punched her in the face, knocking her out. Worf was struggling to his feet when the doors opened at Engineering.

A surprised Geordi La Forge stared at them. "Worf! What happened?"

The Klingon whispered, "Forget that request for more speed." Then he slumped to the floor.

Geordi pressed his badge. "La Forge to sickbay. I need Dr. Crusher in Engineering!"

Worf sat on a table in sickbay. "I am all right," he told Beverly Crusher. His voice, indeed, was strong again. "Just make sure that Shana Russel is watched every minute. As soon as she is able, she is headed for a cell."

Worf tried to shake the tightness from his shoulders. He had won, he told himself. He had caught her. She wouldn't murder again; the contamination was ended.

He pressed his badge. "Worf to Picard."

"Picard here," answered the captain. There was worry in his voice. "Geordi told us what happened. Are you all right?"

"She is the killer, Captain," said Worf. "Shana Russel killed Lynn Costa and Karn Milu. She wanted to ruin Emil Costa. Her mother was Megan Terry—"

"You rest, Lieutenant," ordered the captain. "Shana Russel will be sent to the starbase. Make your report when you are able."

"Yes sir," answered Worf. He grinned as he whispered, "This time, it's certain."

Emil Costa walked back and forth in his cell on

Kayran Rock. What was happening, he wondered.

He was surprised when the outer door opened. Captain Picard, Commander Data, and Kwalrak, the female Kreel, walked toward him.

The captain was smiling. Even the android looked pleased. "Dr. Costa," began Picard, "you will be happy to know that the murder charges against you have been dropped. Shana Russel has confessed to both murders."

"Shana Russel!" he gasped.

"Her name is really Jasmine Terry," explained Data. "She is Megan Terry's daughter. And, she says you are her father."

"Megan—" cried the white-haired scientist.

"You can see the report later," said Picard gently. "Now you must talk with First Assistant Kwalrak. The Kreel still have charges against you from the shuttlecraft incident. They are willing to let you serve five years on this starbase. You must agree to teach science classes to young Kreel.

"We want to learn things for ourselves," said Kwalrak. "We don't want to depend on others. And we know that Dr. Costa has a fine understanding of transporter technology."

"You won't be doing the work for them," Picard told the doctor. "You'll be teaching."

The old scientist looked at Data. "You're my lawyer. Should I take this deal?"

"If you feel you can live inside this asteroid for five years, you should take the deal."

Emil stood up. "I accept," he said.

Captain Picard nodded to the security officer. "Let him go."

A small bell rang. The old man reached out to make sure the force field was gone. He stepped from the cell and shook Data's hand. "Thank you!"

"Do not thank me," said the android. "Thank Lieutenant Worf and Counselor Troi."

Deanna was walking down a hall. *Imagine,* she thought, *sweet little Shana Russel, a cold-blooded killer.*

Suddenly a strong hand took her arm. She turned to see the smiling face of Commander Riker.

"Where are you going?" he asked.

"To the bridge."

"No, you're not!" He turned her toward the turbolift. "You're going to Kayran Rock with me. We're on shore leave!"

A surprised smile crossed Deanna's face. She skipped into step beside him. "How long can we be gone?"

"I figure we'll stay until they come after us," laughed Will.

Lieutenant Worf, Commander Data, and Captain Picard were all in position on the bridge. The door slid open and a smiling Wesley Crusher joined them.

"Report, Lieutenant Worf," ordered Picard.

"In position over Kayran Rock," answered the Klingon. "The last shore leave will end in ten hours. We are cleared to leave at that time."

"Lieutenant," said Jean-Luc, "it's good to see you on the bridge again."

"Captain," he nodded. "It's good to be back."

"As for the job you did while you were away," the captain went on, "I have one thing to say."

"Yes, sir?" asked Worf.

"Well done."